RELUCTANT BUMPKIN

SAM CHEEVER

ELECTRIC PROSE PUBLICATIONS

She's just a girl with a dog, a cat, and a pig. And since she's been drafted into helping her boyfriend scare his younger brother straight, she's a girl who's suddenly glad she's an only child.

Hal's younger brother has been banished to Deer Hollow because of his proclivity for getting into trouble. Hal's parents are hoping he'll take the kid under his wing and straighten him out. But Asher Amity has a knack for finding trouble, and it doesn't take him long to find it in Deer Hollow. When Asher steps into a steaming pile of murder and treachery,

Hal and Joey are destined to get dragged into the mess with him. Who knew how dangerous babysitting could be?

1

G one, gone, gone were the days I wished I had a sibling.

Nope. They weren't just gone...they were obliterated.

I stood with my arms crossed over my chest, my back pressed against the front door of my house, and stared down at the young Greek god with the decidedly ungodlike snarl on his perfect lips. The kid had a "bad boy" air that seemed too big for his years.

Facing off with the mini-Greek god, the full-sized version, who certainly could have been a bad boy if he hadn't worked so hard in his life to prove to others that he wasn't *that guy*, stood with hands on hips and perfect face formed into stone. "Why didn't they tell me they were bringing you?" Hal asked his younger brother, Asher Amity.

The *they* he referred to was their parents, who'd

apparently done the dump and run while Hal and I had been at the grocery buying stuff for dinner. Beside me on the porch, my sweet blonde, green-eyed pitty, Caphy, vibrated like a laundry spin cycle, her deadly tail whipping the wood planking behind her. She was so excited to meet the newcomer she could barely stand it. Pitty-full whining emerged from her throat, and she kept jumping to her feet and then plopping back down when I wouldn't let her leap off the porch and fly into Asher's arms.

I was pretty sure the dark-eyed hostility the kid was flinging around like holy water in a room full of vampires was a good indication he wouldn't appreciate a chest full of pibl.

Asher shrugged, his speculative gaze sliding to me. "They forced me into the car and drove me here. Trust me, brah, if I'd known they were bringing me out to Bumpkinville, I'd have opened the car door and flung myself out onto the highway." His lips curled in disgust as he looked around. "Anything would be better than this place."

A growl vibrated on the air, and it hadn't come from Caphy.

Hal's hands fisted. He took a step back as if afraid he'd pop the brat on the nose. "First of all, you owe Joey an apology for insulting her and her home..."

I opened my mouth to say he didn't. The last thing I wanted was to be inserted into the battle of wills going on at the bottom of the steps.

Hal's gaze whipped my way. The look in his eyes murdered my objection before I could give it life.

Alrighty then.

"Why? It's true," Asher snarled.

"Only a spoiled little brat would look down his nose at this beautiful house," Hal growled. "You'd be lucky to live in this house. Anybody would be. And this town is filled with wonderful people. Just because they live a different kind of life than you're used to doesn't make them bad people. When did you become such a snob?"

Asher's lip curled higher. "It stinks here. Does she have pigs or something?"

I winced. Yep, I did. Well, one pig, anyway. Ethel Squeaks. But that kid had better be careful how he talked about sweet Ethel. Hal loved that pig almost as much as he loved Caphy and...um...me.

"That's manure, genius. The farmers spread it on the fields as fertilizer. You'd know that if you weren't such a city-slicker."

If Hal had meant that term as an insult, it didn't land that way. Asher's back straightened and he raised his perfect Greek nose. "And proud of it."

Hal shook his head, scrubbing a hand over his mouth in frustration. He made a visible attempt to calm himself before speaking to his brother again. "I don't know why mom and dad brought you here, but I can guess. Did you get in trouble again?"

The kid shoved his hands into the pockets of

jeans that hung so low on his narrow hips I was pretty sure a good sneeze would create a denim puddle on the ground. I chewed my bottom lip at those jeans, wondering if the kid had some kind of eating disorder. Surely Hal's parents could afford to buy him jeans that fit. Although, I guessed a seventeen-year-old would probably refuse to let his mom pick out his clothes.

No, the jeans, the boxers I could see sticking up from their too-big waistline, and the tattered black tee-shirt that read "Thug Life" on the front were definitely meant to serve as a statement.

"Maybe we could go inside," I suggested in a voice that was embarrassingly hesitant. I cleared my throat as the two men ripped twin hostile glares in my direction and bent my lips in a stiff smile. "I made fresh lemonade this morning."

Asher snorted derisively, and Hal cuffed him on the back of the head.

"Show respect, or I'll personally drop you into a pile of manure." Hal jerked his head toward the door. "Inside."

Asher slumped up the steps, his spotless white leather sneakers slapping the surface as he ascended.

Still quivering like a jellyfish, Caphy bounced off the porch, barking with excitement. The kid jerked to a stop as if he'd just noticed her. He eyed my pibl for a long moment, his familiar green eyes narrowing.

"This is Caphy," I told him. Offering my hand, I stepped forward. "I'm Joey."

For an uncomfortably long moment, Asher seemed intent on ignoring my hand, but Hal cleared his throat almost violently and the kid huffed out a put-upon breath. He clasped my hand briefly, his own moist with nerves.

My heart softened a little. The kid had been unceremoniously dumped in an alien environment, and he was understandably upset about it.

"Cool dog," he said.

And suddenly, I knew he and I were going to get along famously. Or, at least a little. "She's very sweet," I told him. I released some of the tension on the leash, so the pibl could get closer to our hostile visitor.

Caphy danced forward, tail whipping, body wagging, and tongue lolling on a wide doggy grin.

"She gets a little excited sometimes, though," I finished.

Asher rubbed a hand over Caphy's wide head and she melted beneath his touch.

Hal wrapped an arm around my waist, providing a united front while addressing his brother. "While you're here, you'll treat Joey and the animals with care and respect. Do you understand?"

The kid stiffened, his bottom lip jutting with irritation. He didn't respond, but he didn't argue either, and as he stepped toward the door, Caphy fell in with him, pressing against his thigh as if they'd been friends forever.

Asher opened the front door. I released Caphy's leash so she could follow him inside.

I looked up at Hal, my brows peaking.

He sighed. "Sorry, honey. I'll call my dad and find out what's going on."

I nodded, laying my head on his shoulder. "It's okay. I'm sure they have a good reason for leaving him with...um...you."

His lips curved upward, his dark green gaze sparking with humor. "Oh no you don't, Joey Fulle. We're in this together."

I laughed. "Who says?"

He lowered his lips to mine, the kiss warm and lingering. My knees melted. By the time he broke the kiss a moment later, I was struggling to remember my name.

"You wouldn't desert me in my hour of need, would you?" he murmured huskily.

Not after that kiss. "My assistance can be bought," I told him, grinning.

"Oh yeah?" he asked, tugging me close again. "For the price of another kiss?"

I blew a raspberry. "Not a chance, bud. We're talkin' banana cream pie. Lots of it."

Chuckling softly, Hal tapped my nose. "You drive a hard bargain."

"Yeah, I know. But that's my offer, take it or leave it."

Hal's eyes sparkled. He heaved a dramatic sigh. "Okay. If that's the best I can do..." He held out a hand, and I took it. "It's a deal." Then he yanked me in for another kiss.

Dang! What was my name again?

***

We nearly bumped into Asher when we came through the door. He'd gone very still, his gaze on the tiny pig staring at him from a few feet away.

Ethel Squeaks stared back, her black button eyes unwavering as if assessing whether he was friend or foe. Her new red ball sat in front of her on the slick tile, and her tail spun slowly, showing her uncertainty.

"This is Ethel Squeaks", I told Asher.

His head jerked in my direction as if I'd alarmed him. "You keep a pig in the house?"

His tone, somewhere between disbelief and derision, made Hal stiffen. I squeezed his hand, urging him to give his brother time.

"Yes. She's a pot-bellied pig. She lives here."

Asher's gaze slid back to Ethel. "Is she house trained?"

"Mostly." Hal and I shared a look. "She can use a litter box, but mostly she goes outside."

The kid's stance softened slightly.

Ethel's tail sped.

"Hm."

I had no idea what *Hm* meant, but it didn't seem overly hostile. "She's very sweet," I told him. It seemed I was saying that a lot. But it was true. All my animals were sweet. Skeerrcch! Full stop on that thought. I'd momentarily forgotten LaLee, my opinionated Siamese cat.

Oh well, two out of three ain't bad.

He frowned. "I'm sorry about the pig remark earlier."

"It's okay."

Hal opened his mouth, probably to argue that it wasn't okay at all. I shot him a look.

Ethel lowered her snout and shoved the red ball, sending it rolling toward Asher.

"She wants you to play with her," Hal said.

Asher turned a disbelieving glance his way, barking out a dismissive laugh. "Yeah, sure."

"It's true," I told him. I grabbed Caphy's leash before she could go for the ball. "Ethel loves to play ball."

Asher lifted a dark eyebrow. Ever so slowly, he

stretched his leg and tapped the ball with his toe, sending it rolling back her way.

Ethel's tail spun like a windmill in a tornado. Her tiny hooves tapped the floor, and she ran to meet the rolling ball, bumping it with her snout.

Asher's responding laugh was filled with surprise. "That's a hoot."

"She *is* a hoot," I told him. "I'll get us a snack." As I headed toward the kitchen, the pibl hot on my heels and still dragging her leash, I heard Asher laugh again, followed by the sound of Ethel skidding across the floor and her ball smacking against the wall.

I smiled. Yes, I did have a pig or something. Well, Hal and I had a pig. We were in a co-parenting situation.

And Ethel Squeaks reminded us every single day why we were blessed.

We had lemonade and freshly baked chocolate chip cookies on the back porch. Caphy and Ethel Squeaks had already eaten their bowls of fruit and were running around the yard, chasing each other.

A soft breeze skittered over us, the hot sun blocked by the roof of the porch, and the air was cool, with a slight tang that told me a storm was brewing not all that far away.

The back yard was an acre of grass in the form of rolling hills that were dotted with mature trees and a copse of old-growth evergreens that lent the air the sweet smell of crushed pine needles.

My favorite childhood swing hung from one of the big old trees, a tire on chains that my best friend, Lis and I had spent hours draped over, talking about boys.

Asher devoured his cookies and had three glasses of lemonade. He might stick his nose up at Deer Hollow, but so far he'd been all-in on country visitor traditions.

"You didn't bring anything with you?" Hal asked his brother after we'd finished our snack. "No clothes? Electronics?"

Asher shrugged. "My bag is in the bushes upfront."

My brows lifted into my hairline. "The bushes? Why?"

Asher stared at the animals playing around the evergreen trees, his expression mulish.

"Because he'd been planning to make a run for it before we knew he was here," Hal said, answering for his sibling.

Asher didn't deny the charge.

"Then why didn't you go?" I asked him. I tried to

keep the irritation from my voice but didn't entirely succeed.

The kid's gaze slid farther afield, to the building that was barely visible through the trees. The oversized metal structure had once been used as a hangar for my father's small plane. Silence extended between us, and I realized he wasn't going to answer. I glanced at Hal.

"Asher, Joey asked you a question."

The teen slowly turned to me, his expression filled with rage, his jaw tight. "Because you got here too fast. But don't worry, I'm still planning on leaving."

None of us spoke for a long moment. Finally, Hal nodded. "Okay. I'm not your jailor. If you want to leave, then leave."

Asher blinked in surprise.

I was surely mistaken in my impression that the teen was disappointed by his older brother's declaration. "Good," he finally said.

Hal nodded. "But why don't you give us a couple of nights. Just through the weekend. You might as well enjoy Deer Hollow for a bit before you hit the road."

I tensed, waiting for the kid to scoff at the idea that he might enjoy anything at all about my home.

To my surprise, after a moment's hesitation, Asher nodded. "Okay." He stood up, pointing toward the outbuilding. "What's that?"

"My father had a small plane when he was alive. That's where he stored it."

Asher stared at it for another moment. Then he turned to me. "Can I go check it out?"

"I don't see why not." I stood. "I'll show you around." I glanced at Hal. "You can make your phone calls. We'll be back in a while."

Hal held my gaze for a moment and then nodded. He reached out and gave my hand a quick squeeze. "Thanks." He was thanking me for more than the tour I was about to give the kid. I knew that. I smiled and nodded. "Any time. I'm thinking maybe we should go into town for dinner later."

Hal's smile stretched wide. "And pie?"

Twisting my lips to keep from grinning, I tried to look surprised by the suggestion. "What a good idea. I hadn't even considered it."

2

Asher and I fell into an easy silence as we walked along the grass path toward the back. Caphy and Ethel Squeaks scurried in and out of the tall grasses on either side of the trail, happy as a pig in a mud puddle to explore the great untamed wilderness of our back acreage. Usually, I didn't let them spend much time back there because of the coyotes that were thick in the area. But it was early enough in the day that I didn't think we needed to worry about the predators.

Asher grinned at their antics and even laughed out loud a couple of times, forgetting himself.

Caphy bounded out of the overgrown meadow ahead of us, whipping around to watch the softly swaying blades of grass for the arrival of her adventure buddy. Her muscular body vibrated with excitement, and her tail whipped happily behind her. She bounced excitedly, butt up and tongue lolling, as a blade of grass in front of her shifted sideways.

I touched Asher's arm and he stopped, looking at me with a frown. "Watch this," I whispered.

Unseen by my pibl, the grasses close to Asher and me gently swayed. We watched the passage of our unseen visitor toward the open grass where we stood. Ahead of us, Caphy bounced and whined, her head cocking with concern when her victim didn't immediately emerge to be trounced.

I covered my mouth as a giggle tried to break free. The grass split beside Asher, and Ethel gave us a look, her ears happily twitching. She slipped from the cover of the tall grass, staying close enough to reduce her profile, and walked quietly toward the waiting pibl.

Caphy bounced once, lowering her front end in a playful position as if trying to entice the pig from the grass.

Beside me, Asher laughed softly as he watched it unfold.

"Caphy is the world's worst hunter," I whispered.

Asher's grin was reflected in his dark green gaze.

The pig moved to within ten feet of the pibl and stopped, then opened her snout and gave a loud squeal.

Caphy yelped and jumped into the air. Ethel took off after her, and Caphy jumped into motion, running happy zoomies through the tall grass, occasionally exploding onto the path and returning to the tall grass with bouncing leaps.

Ethel stood in the path and squealed happily every time Caphy hit the shorter grass.

Asher was laughing so hard tears slid from his eyes. His laughter was infectious. I found myself wiping tears off my cheeks too.

"Those two are idiots," he finally said.

"They love each other," I agreed. "An odd couple for sure."

The two animals finally slowed, Caphy panting from her efforts, and we fell into a leisurely stroll behind them. "Have you always lived here?" Asher asked. "In this town? This house?"

I nodded, nostalgia bringing unexpected tears. "Yep. I'm a bumpkin through and through."

His smile slid away. "I didn't mean anything by that."

"Don't worry about it," I said. "I take it as a badge of honor. I love this place. These people." I laughed. "I'm pretty sure Ethel Squeaks wouldn't fit in if I lived in Indianapolis."

He shoved his hands into his pockets and we walked on. After a while, he asked, "Don't you get bored?"

"Bored? Not a chance. There's a ton of stuff to do around here."

"Name five things." His tone was demanding, but I saw the amusement in his gaze.

"Five, huh? Okay." I thought about it for a minute. It would be hard to whittle it down to only five. But there were a few things that formed the basis of every other thing. Finally, I went with the five strongest. "1. Eat banana cream pie. 2. Enjoy gorgeous sunsets. 3. Hike through my woods with Caphy. 4. Commit carb on carb crime."

His brows lifted on that one.

"You'll see later when we go into town for dinner." I thought hard about my fifth thing. I finally settled. "5. Have shared history, memories, and concerns with the people around me. I probably should have put that first. It's really important. Almost everyone who lives in Deer Hollow has lived here all their lives. That means they're invested in this place. They care about keeping it the way it is. There's a lot of comfort in that."

Asher seemed to be considering my words. After a moment, he nodded. "I get that, I guess. I've never felt really at home in any of the places where we've lived. I've never had real friends. Not the kind that understood me at more than a superficial level."

His statement was both sad and surprisingly intuitive for his age. I fought an urge to give him a hug. "You understand then."

He nodded. He understood. And I couldn't help thinking that it surprised him a little.

The hangar loomed ahead of us. As it had since my dad had crashed his little plane on the grass runway, which was now a tangle of weeds, grass, and small trees, a pang of sadness twisted in my belly at the sight.

"Is the plane still in there?" Asher asked.

I pulled air into my lungs, fighting tears. "No. My dad crashed it."

He didn't say anything. I got the sense he was trying to figure out what to say.

I pointed to the mess of weeds and small trees. "Believe it or not, this used to be a grass runway."

His eyes widened. "They landed on grass?" He said it as if the idea were completely foreign to him.

I nodded. "Yep. Of course it didn't look like this at the time."

"How did he crash?"

I swallowed hard. "He hit a big rock as he was landing." I didn't tell him the rock had been put there by someone who wanted my dad dead. Asher didn't need to know that.

"So, you're an orphan?"

I gave a moment's thought to telling him my mom was still alive, but the need to protect her won out over the desire to share. I simply nodded. For all intents and purposes, I *was* an orphan.

He stopped beside the big building, his gaze sliding over its sun-faded walls. There was an emotion on his face I couldn't identify.

I didn't say anything, giving him his moment.

I turned at the sound of Caphy scratching at the door. She glanced up and whined softly.

I stiffened, remembering the last time Caphy had whined at that door.

"What's wrong?" Asher asked, moving closer to me.

I wasn't sure if his action was protective of me or a sign of his own fear. Though, I couldn't imagine what seventeen-year-old Asher Amity would know about fear.

"Nothing. I just had a flashback about something." I smiled up at him. "Ghosts from the past."

He looked like he would ask me more questions I didn't want to answer, so I went into distraction mode. "Do you want to see inside?"

"Could I?"

"Absolutely."

I retrieved the key I'd taped to the underside of the big fuel tank and unlocked the door. Caphy and Ethel Squeaks slipped past me as soon as the door creaked open. The smell of dust and rodent droppings hit me as I followed them inside.

I wrinkled my nose, remembering a time when the smell had been much worse. Once a vagrant had lived in the office of the building. I hadn't known he was there. I also hadn't known he was tied to my family in surprising ways.

The memory had me stopping beside the office door, peering inside. My gaze slid to the lighter square of wall near the window. It was the spot where a small painting of my father's plane had once hung. That painting hadn't been as it seemed either.

Caphy snuffled around the empty desk and in the corner, where once a sleeping bag had served as the focal point for a mountain of junk food debris.

"This place is huge," Asher said, pulling me from my thoughts.

I turned, forcing a smile onto my face. "It is." I rubbed my arms as the Spector of old memories slid over me.

"It's a shame it's sitting empty."

I stared out over the enormous space. In my mind, I was seeing a tidy building with pristine rolling tool carts and my father's pride and joy, a well-kept two-person Cessna, burnished with love.

I'd spent countless hours there as a kid, playing in the big building. The Cessna had seemed enormous then, and I'd been obsessed with it because my dad had been obsessed.

Little had I known it would one day be the instrument of his death. Used against him to remove him forever from my life.

"Have you ever thought of doing something with it?"

I jerked from my depressing thoughts and looked up at Asher. "What?"

He swung a hand to indicate the building. "Were you planning on using this for anything?"

I blinked in surprise. "Uh, no, not really."

He nodded thoughtfully.

I left him to wander around and check the space out for a few minutes and went back outside.

He emerged fifteen minutes later, his handsome young face wearing a thoughtful expression.

I threw the stick I'd been using to entertain Caphy and watched her bound gleefully after it. Ethel was digging at the base of a small scrub tree, going for its succulent roots.

I looked up as Asher joined me. "Ready to head back?"

He nodded.

I locked the building back up, replaced the key, and called my little darlings back to us. We walked in silence all the way back. Even Caphy and Ethel Squeaks were subdued, either reacting to my melancholy or anticipating their upcoming dinner.

Hal was waiting for us on the porch when we entered the yard. From a distance, his expression looked dire. But he smiled as I climbed the steps and wrapped me in a hug. Somehow he'd sensed how the visit to the past had affected me. "Everything okay?"

I nodded.

"That's a cool building," Asher said, his eyes alight.

His enthusiasm surprised me. To anyone who hadn't lived my history, the former hangar must just seem like a big, messy, and slightly neglected structure with no purpose.

I didn't ask Hal what he'd learned from his phone call. If he wanted to speak about it in front of Asher, I knew he would.

"I'll just feed the kids," I told him. "Then we can head into town."

He nodded, his gaze sliding speculatively toward Asher, and I left them alone to talk. Or not.

3

Silence pulsed from the back seat of Hal's big SUV. I imagined I felt waves of judgment coming from the silent teen back there.

I tried to imagine how the small town would appear to a kid who considered himself too cool for country. I gave up after a few minutes. I didn't want to see Deer Hollow that way. I loved it too much to see it in a poor light, even in an attempt to view it through someone else's eyes.

As we passed the town's only daycare center, *Brats versus Broads,* I was pretty sure I heard Asher snicker. The massive sign for the daycare showed a cartoonish female character with long dark hair. She was wearing superhero garb and wielding a whip. Facing off with the "Broad" was a masked baby in a diaper that was covered in stars and stripes and pointing a bottle that shot lightning bolts at his nemesis. I grinned. Politically correct we were *not* in Deer Hollow. And I found it endlessly entertaining.

Sonny's Diner was located in the exact center of Deer Hollow's main street. The spokes of road jutting off Main were too short to be considered real roads. But each one hosted an assortment of small-town businesses mixed with single-family homes along their abbreviated lengths.

Sonny's had been established by a guy named Matthew Earl. He'd been a selfish, surly only child who was spoiled rotten by his mother, and she'd called him Sonny his entire life for no explicable reason.

The current owner of the diner was Sonny's daughter, Max. The humble little diner squatted under a massive sign promising the best banana cream pie in the state. Max delivered on that promise.

I didn't look at Asher as we stepped into the restaurant. In that moment, I was afraid his disdain for the homey place might make me like him less.

Max lifted her gaze when the bell on the door jangled and jutted her chin toward the dining room. "Sit wherever you want," she called out in a gravelly voice. "Verna'll be with ya in a minute."

I headed toward my favorite booth on the back wall. The red vinyl covering on the booth's bench seats had cracked several times over the years and had been repaired with ill-matching red tape. I took care as I slid into one side, not to let the cracked vinyl scratch my legs.

In honor of Asher's visit, and maybe secretly because I was sensitive to the whole bumpkin thing despite what I'd told the kid, I'd donned a pretty sundress and sandals with a little heel instead of my usual shorts and flip flops.

Asher still wore his thug fashion, a fact that had earned him several disapproving stares on the way into the diner.

Hal slid in beside me, looking gorgeous and very Hal-like in dark jeans and a crisp white button-up shirt. No flip flops for my PI. His sandals were a classy leather and looked good on his big, perfect feet.

Verna came out of the kitchen and grabbed menus from the front podium by the door before heading our way. As usual, her dark hair pouffed around her face, disrupted in its pouffiness only by the pencil stuck behind her ear.

She popped her gum as she stopped beside our table, giving Hal and me a welcoming smile before scanning Asher a curious glance.

"Verna, this is my brother, Asher," Hal said.

Verna nodded at the teen. "Charmed."

Asher frowned as if trying to discern the meaning in Verna's greeting. "Hey."

"What can I get you to drink?" Verna asked, tugging the pencil from her hair.

"Do you have beer?" Asher asked.

Three pairs of eyes slid his way, none of them supportive of his choice.

"Try again, junior," Hal said.

"I'll just have water," I said quickly when Asher bristled.

"Same," Hal said. He jerked his head at his brother. "The upstart there will have a Coke."

Verna's lips twitched as she turned away to get our drinks.

Asher glared at Hal.

"Don't give me attitude," Hal told the kid. "You're seventeen. In case you missed it, the legal age for drinking here in Indiana is still twenty-one."

"Nobody would have cared if you'd have just gone along with it," Asher ground out.

"Why would I do that?" Hal asked. "That's the type of poor decision making that has always gotten you into trouble."

"I see you've still got that giant stick up your a..."

"What sounds good for dinner?" I asked, interrupting Asher.

Both men slid angry gazes my way. I narrowed my eyes at Hal, and he took a deep breath. "Sorry. You're right. Let's just try to enjoy dinner." He addressed his words to Asher.

To my surprise, the kid picked up his menu, letting go of the argument.

Something in my chest loosened. I'd been pretty

sure we were going to have to take our food and our battles to go.

"What's the carb-on-carb crime you were talking about?" Asher asked.

I grinned. "Chicken and noodles served over mashed potatoes."

He gave me a smile that was enough like his older brother's to charm me. "I'll have that."

I nodded. "You have to get it with green beans in a nod to good nutrition."

He shrugged.

"And follow it up with banana cream pie."

The kid's eyes lit up. "I'm starting to see why you call it that."

Verna came back with our drinks and we ordered. Asher and I got chicken and noodles. Hal got the roast chicken special.

I opened my mouth to tell her we wanted pie, but she cut me off. "I already have three slices set aside for you." Verna didn't smile, but she gave me a wink before heading to the kitchen to put our orders in.

We sat in uncomfortable silence for a beat. All three of us turned toward the door as it opened, the bell jangling happily.

Arno Willager, my friend Lis' favorite villager, walked through the door. His intense brown gaze slid through the restaurant, cataloging the diners. It landed on us and he started forward. His gaze turning speculative when he spotted Asher.

At six feet two, Deputy Willager was two inches shorter than Hal and he was light where Hal was dark, as you'd expect with his Greek heritage. Arno's blond hair was slightly unkempt as usual, the pale highlights a natural effect of being out in the sun for a lot of the day. He had broad shoulders and narrow hips, and his long legs quickly ate up the distance between the door and our booth.

Hal stood when he arrived and offered Arno his hand. "Deputy."

Arno let his gaze slide over Asher. "Amity." He looked at me. "Joey."

Even for Arno, who was generally a man of few words, his demeanor was intense and abrupt.

Reading the message in Arno's gaze, Hal indicated Asher with a sweep of his hand. "Deputy Willager, this is my younger brother, Asher. He's staying with us for a couple of days."

Arno offered Asher his hand. The kid stood awkwardly and took it. "Sir."

"It's nice to meet you," Arno told the kid. "You from Indy?"

Asher nodded. "Yes, sir."

Arno gave the teen a long, assessing look and then nodded at me. "It was nice to see you, Joey."

I smelled a rat. "Nice to see you too, Arno. Why

don't we double date again soon? There's a new restaurant in Greenwood Lis and I would like to try."

Arno swung a look my way, crinkles gathering at the corners of his eyes. But his well-shaped lips didn't so much as twitch. "If I can find time in between catching and jailing criminals, I'd like that."

Because Deer Hollow was such a hotbed of crime.

"Good." I grinned. "It's a potential future date of unknown specifics then."

Arno's lips curved. We watched him walk out of the diner, after never even looking at a menu, and I turned to Hal. "That's weird. It was almost as if he was looking for somebody."

Hal ignored me, but I didn't miss the way his fine mouth tightened.

Fortunately for him, Verna chose that moment to deliver our food.

"You had Arno come in to spook him, didn't you?"

We sat on the porch swing at the front of the house, watching Caphy run around the pond looking for hapless turtles and unsuspecting frogs. LaLee was draped over the wide railing, her tail lazily waving behind her and her dark ears perked. The Siamese watched her canine sister with interest but seemed to have zero inclination to join in her messy antics.

Hal glanced over at me, light sparking in his dark gaze. "Yes."

"Why?"

"I wanted him to know that just because things seem lazy and easy here, it doesn't mean he can act any way he wants."

I frowned. "You think he's going to do something bad?"

Hal reached over and clasped my hand, his grip warm and sure. "I haven't told you about the call with my father."

I let that sink in for a moment while I tried to decide how to respond. Hal opened his mouth to continue, but I held up a hand, stopping him. "Before you tell me what you're going to tell me, did you ask your dad why they brought the kid here instead of to your house?"

Hal chuckled softly. "I did. He said they went to my house first, but my car wasn't there. They weren't comfortable leaving him in the middle of the woods where...and I quote...*all manner of wild animals could eat him.*"

I laughed. Hal's and Ash's parents had always lived in the tame and manicured suburbs. To them, the woods where Hal's cozy little cabin lived probably looked like a dark forest from a Brothers Grimm story.

"So they came here," Hal continued. "They knew I spent as much or more time here than at home."

I nodded. "That makes sense." I frowned. "But why the dump and run? Why didn't they stay and talk to us?"

"Dad was vague on that, but I got the sense they're trying to scare the kid straight."

"I'm not sure I like that. I don't exactly live in a prison."

Hal sighed. "That's not a statement on your house or even mine. It was more a case of taking him completely out of his comfort zone and away from the influences that allowed him to get into trouble. Dad's hoping a big brother might have more influence on the kid than his...I'm quoting now...*stupid* parents."

I shook my head. "Okay, I'm ready for the rest."

"Ash got into some trouble in Indy." His eyes met mine. "Bad trouble."

I felt my eyes widen. "How bad can it be?" What I meant was, since the teen was in Deer Hollow instead of jail.

"Really bad."

My pulse sped. "What did he do?"

"Hopefully nothing. But he's been hanging with some guys who may have killed someone."

I choked on nothing, coughing violently for a moment while Hal patted my back unhelpfully. When I could speak again, I asked, "Are we safe?"

"From Asher? Yes. But Dad's worried about Asher's buddies coming to Deer Hollow. I told Arno because I wanted him to be aware of the situation."

"Tell me what happened in Indy."

The front door swung open and Asher came out onto the porch. He'd been watching TV with Ethel Squeaks and his hair was rumpled from the blankets he'd made into a nest on the floor.

"Hey," I said as he stretched and yawned. "Is the movie over?"

In response, he said. "The pig hogged the blanket."

"She has a tendency to do that," Hal said, grinning.

Asher jerked his chin toward the pond. "What's that goofy dog doing?"

"She likes to hunt turtles and frogs," I said, smiling as Caphy jumped on a spot in the grass, tail wagging. As usual, she came up empty.

"Does she ever catch them?" Asher asked.

"Not very often. Though I have come into the house and found box turtles lying upside down on the rug a few times."

"No way!" Asher laughed.

"Way." I shook my head. "She doesn't hurt them. She just likes to carry them around."

The kid sat down on the top step and yawned again.

"You ready to go home?" Hal asked his brother.

"No, I'm good." He stared at Caphy a few more minutes and then sighed. Without looking at Hal, he said. "Dad told you what happened?"

"He did."

Asher's expression was mulish when he turned to us. "Will and Kevin had nothing to do with that girl's death."

"Dad said it was an overdose. He said the police suspect your buddy Will of selling drugs. If he sold that girl the drugs that killed her, he's responsible, Ash."

Hal's tone was gentle. But there was steel beneath the softness.

Asher shook his head. He jammed his hands into the pocket of his hoodie. "Will doesn't do drugs, and he doesn't sell them. They're pinning his brother's crimes on him. It's not fair."

"Tell me about Will's brother," Hal said.

"He's an ex-con. Will's only his half-brother, but Penn's always treated him like a real sibling, ya know?" Asher looked at Hal, seeming to want him to respond.

"Half brother counts as real," Hal said. "It's not always about blood. Sometimes it's just about love."

The sentiment sounded strange coming from the Greek god. But it made me want to wrap myself around him.

Asher seemed to consider it for a moment and then nodded. "Penn made a mistake. He sold oxy for a while on the street. He did his time, and he's trying to make amends. He's always tellin' Will not to get involved in that stuff. He doesn't even want him to drink." Asher wrinkled his nose at the idea like he smelled something bad. "Drinking's harmless."

"Not if you're driving," Hal said, but he nodded when Asher bristled. "But I get your point."

"Anyway, Will drinks a beer now and then. If he didn't, the guys would razz him about being a wuss. But he doesn't want anything to do with drugs. None of us do."

"Tell me about Kevin."

I was watching the kid pretty closely, so I saw when his shoulders stiffened. A muscle worked in his cheek as he kicked at a small rock near his feet. "Kev's different. I don't really like him all that much. He's really Will's friend. Well, he was, anyway."

"Why don't you like him?" I asked, just because I was curious.

Asher shrugged. "Kev and I are like oil and water."

"Could he have sold the drugs instead of Will?"

Asher shook his head but didn't give reasons for his rejection of the idea. He jumped to his feet. "I'm gonna go see what the dog's up to."

LaLee watched the teen go, her body tense and her tail twitching energetically like it did when she was uncomfortable with someone or something.

Not too surprisingly, she hadn't let Asher warm

up to her. The Siamese cat had a prickly personality. She didn't like change, and she didn't appreciate strangers. Asher would have to work to gain her trust, and I doubted he was interested in doing it. He seemed happy to interact with Ethel and Caphy.

Hal sighed, his thigh flexing as he pressed his foot against the wood planks to start the swing swaying.

"There's more to that story," I said softly.

"Yeah," Hal agreed. "There is."

"Is Arno checking into the girl's death?"

"It's a delicate line for him to walk," Hal said, frowning. "Since it's an ongoing investigation, he needs the IMPD detective in charge to invite him in. Otherwise, he can't do much more than request information-sharing."

"Will he do that?"

Hal finally turned to me. His eyes looked haunted in the moonlight. "If he does, he'll have to tell them why. The IMPD will take a closer look at Asher if they sense Arno's worried about him. I'm not ready to put that kind of spotlight on Ash. Not until I know he's earned it."

I laid my head on Hal's shoulder. I didn't want to ask the question on my mind but knew I needed to. "What if he was involved in the girl's death?"

Hal stopped the swing with his toe, and alarm streaked through me. Had I offended him with my question? I lifted my head and stared into his eyes.

His jaw was tight, but he didn't look angry. He leaned in and kissed my forehead, the touch of his lips almost an apology. "I shouldn't have dragged you into this. I'll take Asher back to Indy tomorrow and stay there until we can get to the bottom of it."

I shook my head. "I don't want you to do that. I think he'll talk to you about things if we give him time. He just needs to realize he's safe here."

Hal held my gaze for a beat and then sighed, dragging me close for a hug. "I don't really believe Ash had anything to do with the girl's death. But if I discover he did...I'll turn him in to the police myself."

It was what I'd expected him to say. It was true to his nature and values.

So why did it make me feel so sad?

4

I was back on the front porch swing when Hal's black SUV drove down my drive the next morning and pulled into the circular drive. I stood up and bounced down the steps to the car as Hal came around the big vehicle and opened my door. He gave me a lingering kiss. "Morning, beautiful."

Heat flared through me, and I realized we probably had an observer. "Mornin'. Did everybody sleep okay?"

Hal stepped back and I slipped inside the car.

"The pig hogged the covers again," the inhabitant of the back seat groused.

Hal slid behind the wheel. "Ash thought it would be a great idea to sleep on the floor in front of the fireplace last night. Esther kept absconding with his stuff."

I turned to look at Asher in the back seat. "Did she cart them all to her tent?"

He tried to look disgusted, but I saw the telltale spark of amusement in his eyes. "Yeah. What's up with that? She took the TV clicker about five times. She also kept stealing my shoe and that little throw pillow from the chair. She took the pillow right out from under my head twice. I even had to hide my phone on the mantle because she kept trying to steal that."

I laughed. "It's a pig thing, I guess. She's the first pig I've had. But all her treasures go into the tent. She's a hoarder."

"I couldn't find my keys last week. They were buried in her tent," Hal offered, grinning.

Asher shook his head and stared out the window.

"You didn't bring her back," I said to Hal.

"I offered her a car ride, but she was tired and didn't want to come. She ate her breakfast and went right back to bed."

I frowned. "I hope she's okay."

"She's fine," Hal said. "She's just worn out from being up all night torturing Ash."

A heartfelt sigh filled the back seat.

"Where are you taking us for breakfast?" I asked my PI.

He grinned. "It's a surprise."

He was certainly right about that. I was very

surprised when we pulled into my best friend Lis's driveway and parked.

I arched my eyebrows at Hal.

He grinned. "It was her idea. She wants to meet Asher."

The kid sighed again, the weight of the world on his bony, teenaged shoulders.

My lips curved upward. He was expecting to be surrounded by "old" people and bored out of his mind. I couldn't wait until he got a look at Lis.

If he was a normal red-blooded male, he'd be anything but bored.

I gave the property a look as we walked along the freshly paved drive. The rock garden the previous owner had put in was still there. Lis had taken the unkempt borders of the garden and given them form. She'd also added a few ornamental trees and bushes that gave the garden more color.

We followed one of the pathways created by different colored stones and slate pavers between raised flower beds and the occasional twisty bush or decorative tree. A fountain and pond were the centerpieces of the space, the water splashing gently over a complex array of differently-sized and shaped rocks.

Koi fish swam and darted in the watery depths of the architecturally appealing fountain.

On the small front porch, Lis had added large pots on either side of the freshly painted aqua-colored front door. The pots and the arrangements continued the Japanese motif that had no doubt inspired the rock garden. I stopped to admire the beautiful mix of Asiatic lilies, birds of paradise galax leaves, some type of red berry, and bamboo-like canes that gave the display form.

I liked the changes Lis had made since moving in. Her talent with color and style was just one more thing at which my friend excelled.

When Lis had left her old career behind and decided to begin a new one in Deer Hollow, she'd been lucky enough to replace her deceased predecessor at Deer Hollow Realtor, in both her job and her residence.

She hadn't inherited the realtor's cat, however. LaLee had found a home with Caphy and me.

Hal knocked on the door and Lis's voice rang out from inside. "Come in!"

My nose twitched as I led the way through the door. I moaned at the delicious scent of bacon and the sweet aroma of cinnamon and pastry. "Please tell me you made your prize-winning monkey bread," I said on a groan. My stomach rumbled loudly in reaction to the decadent scents.

Lis closed her oven door and turned, a frilly white apron tied around her slim waist, June Cleaver style. She grinned widely, shoving a strand of auburn hair out of her eyes. Since becoming a realtor, Lis had cut her once long and silky locks into a short, perky pixie that showed off her fine features and smoky blue gaze.

Beneath the apron, she wore a form-fitted running top and matching capris pants. "I also made feta and spinach omelets!" she announced with pride.

"That sounds delicious. I'm starving."

A shoe scuffed over the wooden floor behind me, and I heard a sharp intake of air. I smiled. Without turning, I said. "Ash, this is..."

"Lis Villa," he breathed out. I turned to find him standing in front of the door with his mouth hanging open. He wasn't even blinking.

Lis, who'd long ago grown accustomed to the reaction from men, just laughed. "In the flesh. Hey, Hal," Lis said.

"Morning, Lis. It smells great in here."

I was pretty sure I heard Asher whimper.

"You recognized her," I said to the teen, for no reason except to get the kid to close his mouth and respond. I wanted to make sure he hadn't entered a catatonic state.

Asher nodded, mouth still open.

"Aunt Lis..." A young woman came through the door leading to the back yard. She held a basket filled with flowers over her arm and carried a small pair of clippers in one hand. "The roses were really pretty," the girl said. "So I grabbed some of those too."

Behind me, Asher made a small sound that could have been from pain.

I didn't blame him. The girl was drop-dead gorgeous. Where Lis had a thick cap of silky auburn hair, the younger woman's dark red hair fell in a dense, silky wash well past her shoulders. Her eyes were a lighter blue than Lis's, with an exotic tilt, and outlined by thick arcs of lashes.

She was slender but had all the requisite curves that somehow were only emphasized by the peasant girl shirt tucked into mid-thigh length, frayed denim shorts. Her long, slender feet were bare and the toenails were painted a vibrant red. She grinned at Asher when she spotted him, showing perfect white teeth. "Hey," she said in a slightly husky voice.

Asher cried softly, sounding like an injured raccoon.

I bit my lip to keep from laughing at his reaction. "Bored yet?" I couldn't resist asking softly.

Asher's gaze reluctantly dragged in my direction, and he finally closed his mouth. "Wow."

I patted his shoulder. "Yeah. I guess you've seen some of Lis' work?"

Lis had been a world-famous catalog and runway model before giving it all up for home and friends. And, let's be honest, for the ability to eat sweets and French fries when she felt like it. Not that the food-freedom had done anything to ruin her ridiculously gorgeous body. Good DNA and old habits kept Lis perpetually lithe and slim.

Dang her soul.

The front door opened behind Asher and Arno came inside holding a large bottle of juice in one hand and a bottle of champagne in the other. Lis's gorgeous face turned all gooey at the sight of him. I was pretty sure Arno forgot to breathe for a beat when he spotted her.

The big cop cleared his throat and nodded at me. "Mornin' Joey, Hal."

The men shook hands.

"Asher." Arno offered a hand to Asher and the kid blinked in surprise, finally taking Arno's big paw and giving it a brisk shake.

Lis wrapped her arm around the girl's shoulders, and they descended the single step from the kitchen and joined us in the middle of the living room. "Joey, I think you know Amethyst?"

I gave Lis's younger cousin a smile. "Hey, girl. You've gotten tall since I last saw you."

Amethyst gave me a hug. "It's nice to see you again."

"Hal," this is my cousin, Ame. "She's visiting from Carmel."

Carmel, Indiana was a very nice suburb of Indianapolis.

"It's nice to meet you, Ame. This is Asher," Hal said, nodding a greeting.

Asher cleared his throat and wiped his hands on his jeans. "It's nice to see...erm...meet...um."

Ame gave the poor goof a dazzling smile. "I'm glad to see somebody my own age," she told him. She gave Lis a slightly guilty glance. "Nothing personal, Aunt Lis."

"Yeah," Lis said, snorting. "It's hard to hang out with all us old people. I understand."

Since Lis and I were barely twenty-six, the girl's characterization of us as old was especially hilarious.

"Well, Sonny," Hal said in a perfect impression of an old guy. He slapped Arno on the back. "What say we sit down before we fall down and we can talk about all our aches and pains while the little women put food on the table?"

Arno snorted out a laugh. "Not so fast, paw." He held up the beverages in his hands. "I'm in charge of the Mimosas."

"Mmm," I said. "What's the occasion?"

Lis tossed her head, grabbing my hand. "No occasion. Just good food and good friends. Come on. I want you to taste the hash brown casserole. I'm not sure if it needs more pepper."

I sat back in my chair and sighed happily. My stomach was about as full as it would go, but I was still eyeing that monkey bread. Maybe I could fit one more piece in.

"You can take some home," Lis said, grinning at me. "You'll save me from eating it."

I gave her back a grin of my own. "It was delicious," I told her. And it was. If I didn't love her so much, I'd hate her for being so perfect.

"Outstanding." Arno fixed Lis with a look that would have boiled the eggs if they'd been anywhere near the stove. "You outdid yourself."

She laughed, flinging a dismissive hand. "The secret is to get you slightly loopy with mimosas before you eat."

Hal lifted his glass. "These are great too. But the food stands on its own."

Lis did a little half-bow from her seat. "Thank you."

I glanced toward the living room, where Asher and Ame sat on a small, black couch and chatted, their eyes alight with mutual interest. They kept their voices low so we couldn't hear what they were saying, but the teen looked completely transfixed by Ame's words, whatever they were.

"I love the new furniture," I told my friend. "Business must be good at Deer Hollow Realty."

Lis sipped her drink. "It is, actually. The homes in that new subdivision are selling like hotcakes."

I looked at my lap to hide my expression. Like most of the long-time residents of the quaint town, I wasn't a fan of the second new subdivision on the South end of Deer Hollow. Our town resources were already being challenged by the first subdivision. The new one would only make things worse.

Randy Garrett, Deer Hollow's new Mayor, was even talking about adding a traffic light to Main Street.

Sacrilege!

The kids got up and headed out the front door. Hal watched them go and then turned to Arno. "Have you spoken to Detective Muldane?"

I assumed Muldane was the cop in Indianapolis who was running the overdose victim's investigation.

Arno pushed his chair back and crossed his long legs at the ankles. "She's doubtful that Penn Zola is a viable suspect. Zola was playing cards in his buddy's garage when the girl was reputed to have purchased the drugs." He slid a glance toward the front door, frowning. "One of the boys, Kevin Rich, broke his silence when Muldane told him he was looking at prison time if he withheld information."

Arno sat forward. "He gave up the other kid?"

"He did." Arno's gaze slid to Hal's and held. "Unfortunately, Rich implied Will Zola had a partner whose name he didn't share."

Hal's mouth tightened. "Does Muldane think it's Asher?"

"She didn't come out and say that, no, but she was happy to be informed of Asher's current whereabouts. The kid needs to keep a low profile until this is wrapped up in Indy. We don't need Muldane deciding to pull him in because he makes himself a target."

The grim look on Hal's face didn't waver. "I'll talk to him."

Lis sipped her coffee. "I want you to know that Ame's a good kid. She won't get him into any trouble."

Hal glanced up in surprise. "Did I miss something?"

Lis and Arno shared a look. "I already asked Deputy Willager about it," she grinned when Arno shook his head at the title. Unspoken behind it were the words, "Deer Hollow's favorite villager." A not-so-veiled reference to the Village People. Arno would make a great dancing cop. However, if he started to sing, dogs would howl from twenty miles away.

"I told her you wanted the kid to hang around Deer Hollow for a while," Arno told Hal.

"I do."

I couldn't help wondering why Hal looked like he was expecting something to explode?

Lis lost some of her confidence at his reaction,

but she said, "I thought Asher might be more amenable to sticking around if he made friends here."

Hal stared at her for a long moment. She shifted in her seat.

"I think that's a great idea," I told Lis, giving her a smile. I squeezed Hal's arm. "The safest thing for Asher is for him to be here, right?"

Hal stared at his clasped hands on the table.

"It's what your parents want," I offered.

As if some silent communication had passed between them, Lis and Arno got up and started gathering the dirty plates.

I turned in my chair. "Penny for your thoughts?"

Hal squeezed my hand between both of his and sighed. "I just don't know what the right thing to do is. It seems reckless to put the kid who's in trouble because he's made such bad friend choices right back into that situation again."

"I know Ame," I told him, speaking softly. "She's kind and sweet and as straightforward as they come. He couldn't hang out with anyone more grounded."

"I'm not worried about Ame. It's just..."

I read between the worry lines on Hal's face. If Asher and Ame started doing things with other kids, Asher might find trouble in Deer Hollow too. He seemed prone to finding it.

The sound of clanking silverware and dishes

clacking together had me glancing toward the kitchen again.

Arno wrapped his arm around Lis's shoulders, giving her a little squeeze before engaging her in playful banter.

That was the moment I realized how close they'd become. They were in an actual relationship. The realization made me smile.

"What are you smiling about?" Hal asked.

I jerked my chin toward my friends. "They look like a couple."

His gaze followed mine. "Yeah. They do." He smiled too, and I relaxed.

"If you don't want Asher to hang with Ame, we'll put the kibosh on it."

"No. It's not a bad idea. I'm going to have to trust him a little, or this isn't going to work." He stood up and gathered our plates. "Shall we go help?"

"Yes, we shall."

5

We dropped Asher at Hal's house, with a plea to be left alone to "do his thing". Whatever that was. Hal left me at home with a promise to call later. He had some legwork to do for his brother, Cal. The two older Amity brothers owned a private investigation business with clients across the country. The business kept them busy, and I cherished the time Hal was able to spend in Deer Hollow with me.

But that meant I found myself at home with nothing I needed to do. I was technically unemployed, having recently sold off the family farm auction business that had been my father's passion. But between my friends, house, and grounds, as well as helping Hal and Arno with the occasional murder, I rarely found myself bored.

Unfortunately, the murders happened more often than one would expect.

I wasn't really bored. I had lots of stuff I could and should be doing, but the enormous breakfast and the mimosas had left me sleepy.

I briefly considered taking a nap. Then I shoved the thought away and spent some time cleaning and doing laundry. When that was done, I headed outside to add algae chemicals to the pond and pull weeds in the flower beds around the house. By the time I was done with all that, the afternoon sun had baked me into lethargy again. All I wanted was to hide in the house and drink lemonade.

Alas, it wasn't to be.

Having been as patient as she believed she could be throughout the day, Caphy was tired of watching me do chores. She might have enjoyed the pond task if I hadn't had to lock her in the house so she wouldn't eat the chemicals as I scattered them at the water's edge.

When I went back inside, she was all over me, dancing around my feet, whining, and running back and forth from me to the front door. She wanted to go for a walk. I decided I could handle a slow walk in the shade of the trees. Hopefully, it would burn off a few of the calories I'd consumed at breakfast.

"Okay, sweet girl. You talked me into it." I grabbed her leash off the hook in the kitchen and clipped it on.

"Meow?" LaLee asked from the back of the couch.

"We're going for a walk through the woods. Do you want to go?" I asked the opinionated feline.

To my surprise, she jumped off the couch and bounded into the entryway.

I narrowed my gaze on her. "I don't want you running off. Do I need to put a leash on you?"

"Yowl, hssssss!"

I sighed. "Okay, but you need to stick close."

Her response was to jam her dark nose through the crack as I opened the door and bound through before Caphy could beat her out.

The pibl took off like a shot after her. With a frustrated yelp, I let go of the leash before Caphy could yank me right into the edge of the door. "Wait for me, you two!"

I sighed, realizing my sedate stroll through the woods might not work out exactly as I'd hoped.

The sun was high and bright and the day had turned hot. I left Caphy to run free, the leash dragging the ground in case I needed to catch her.

She and her snotty sister explored every tree we passed, teasing the squirrels that chittered angrily from the highest branches.

Unbeknownst to the chirping rodents, LaLee could actually climb the trees if she wanted to. She'd nearly caught one of the squirrels who'd been taunting the pitty from the distant heights of a particularly impressive walnut tree.

Even worse, the cat ignored my shrieking for her to leave the hapless creature alone as only a cat could. After a suitable period of time had passed to prove she was doing it on her own terms, LaLee finally descended the tree, sailing gracefully from branch to branch until she landed lightly in the dirt.

Felines. You couldn't live with them, and you couldn't return them for a refund.

I settled into the walk, blissfully inhaling the sweet, hot air and enjoying the pleasant trills and flutterings of a multitude of birds.

The trees provided enough shade to make the heat bearable, but adequate sun to keep the Grimm's fairytale feeling at bay.

We followed familiar paths that wound up familiar hills and into familiar ravines. After an hour of exploring, the distant sound of the river told me we'd probably better turn back, or I was going to lose one of my frisky companions to the enticement of a cool swim.

The currents in that part of the river were treacherous, and I'd always made it a point to keep Caphy away from it. She got into enough trouble in the pond in front of my house.

As if I'd conjured her from my thoughts, Caphy started barking from somewhere over the next hill.

LaLee had been sharpening her claws on the rough bark of a walnut tree, but her head came up and the lazy waving of her long tail took on a more energetic tone.

The first tendrils of unease tightened my chest.

"Caphy girl, come!"

Caphy continued to bark, the sound growing increasingly strident.

I hurried toward the hill. "Caphy! Come!"

The pitty usually listened to my "mean voice". Unless there was something more interesting to keep her attention.

LaLee sprinted along beside me as I started to run. The hill was one of the larger ones in the woods. When I'd topped the incline, I found myself standing on the edge of a ravine, the sides steep and treacherous. I all but slid down the first side and then had to scramble and grasp at roots and saplings to make it up the opposite slope.

My voice was breathless when I called Caphy again. "Caphy, girl. Come!"

Somewhere around the middle of the upward slope, the pibl had gone quiet. Already at the top of the hill, LaLee yowled unhappily and hissed.

Icy fear made me quicken my steps. What if Caphy had run into a coyote? The thought was terrifying. I'd heard too many stories of pets being lured away by seemingly playful coyotes, only to be attacked in numbers once they'd gotten them alone.

"Caphy!" My voice took on a strident shriek as panic took me completely over.

LaLee suddenly shot away on an angry yowl, and I nearly choked to death trying to find the air to scream as I scrabbled for purchase on the slippery ravine wall. "LaLee, no! Caphy!"

I shoved myself the last couple of feet, my heart pounding like a piledriver and my hands bloodied from the fight to climb.

My frantic gaze slipped over the woods that was laid out in front of me. I spotted a low form shooting through the trees, agile and fast.

I cried out, an unformed sound built of pure fear. Had that been a coyote? *No...please no.*

I started to run, my eyes on the fast-moving form gliding too quickly away from me.

LaLee disappeared into the obscuring branches of a huge evergreen ahead of me. I stepped up my speed, catching my foot in a root and slamming to the ground with a surprised cry.

Ignoring the pain in my knees and palms, I shoved back to my feet and started forward.

Something moved to my right and, before I could see what it was, pain exploded on the side of my head. And the ground roared up to smack me.

6

S oft whining dragged me back to consciousness.
I lay very still for a minute, my mind too muzzy to react. The rich scent of moist earth rose up around me, and birds sang to each other from the branches of nearby trees.

Claws moved over the ground, and the soft chuff of a nervous animal raised the hairs along my arms.

Where was I? Why couldn't I get my brain to work?

I became aware of something poking into my back, and I shifted. A marching band, complete with spiked boots that hit the ground with unnecessary enthusiasm, thundered through my brain.

I went very still, willing the band to take a break.
Get off the field, boys and girls. It's halftime.
I snorted a laugh at the random thought.

Something snuffled through my hair and a wide, wet tongue swiped my face.

I reached out and cupped Caphy's muzzle without opening my eyes. I'd know that whine, snuffle, lick routine anywhere. "Hey, pretty girl." I forced my eyes open to look at her.

Bright red blood coated her head. I jolted in fear and then gave a soft cry as the marching band took up the Star-Spangled Banner and circled the field again.

I moved more slowly, hoping to keep the spikes of pain at bay. "Are you okay?" I asked my dog.

Her response was to lick my face again.

"Come here, girl." I carefully examined her golden fur and found no explanation for the blood. Then I caught a glimpse of my searching hand and gasped.

The blood had come from me!

I carefully touched my temple, finding pain and cooling moisture with my fingertips. "Ouch."

Caphy laid down next to me, plopping her big head on my thigh.

I dropped my head in my hands and prayed the pulsating pain would stop. "What happened?" I asked my dog.

She shifted her muscular body closer and sighed.

I tried to remember how I'd gotten on the ground. Gazing around the spot where I lay, I saw moist churned dirt and a half-dislodged root. The tip of my sneaker was covered in wet earth and my knees were muddy. My legs and arms were covered in scratches, but I was pretty sure I'd gotten those from chasing Caphy through the ravine.

Had I tripped and hit my head?

My mind churned through the visible clues. Yes. I'd been chasing Caphy. I remembered the low forms snaking through the trees and my pulse shot higher. "LaLee!"

Caphy whined. The sound made my pulse pound harder.

"No, no, no!" I murmured, surging upright before I considered what that would do to my head.

"Ouch! Ugh..."

A strident ringing sound pierced the silence. I jumped before realizing it was my phone. I really needed to take the time to get a softer ring tone. I dug into the pocket of my cutoffs and dragged the cell free. It was Hal. "Hey," I croaked.

I tried to climb to my feet but dizziness swamped me and I gave up.

"Joey, oh thank goodness! Where are you?"

I narrowed my gaze on the slice of woods surrounding me. I generally knew my woods like the back of my hand, but my mind was still clogged with fuzz. "Caphy, LaLee, and I took a walk."

"Where, honey? Where did you walk?"

I licked my dry lips. "I'm in the woods."

I heard footsteps through the phone. "Are you on the path?" Hal's voice was slightly breathy as if he were walking fast.

"I was." A fresh wave of agony cut through my poor skull. I wobbled, stars bursting before my eyes. "Caphy was barking, and I saw coyotes."

Charcoal edged my vision. I hit the ground and misery wrenched a short scream from my throat.

"Joey! What happened? Talk to me, honey."

"I..." I swallowed hard. "...thought she was in trouble, so I ran. I think I fell."

"Describe the area for me," he said, his voice husky with concern.

"Trees." My eyelids fluttered. "The walls are st..." I swallowed again, feeling as if I were lying on a boat on the ocean. The ground beneath me rolled and shifted, making me seasick.

Caphy whined again and her tongue found my nostril.

I twitched, pushing her away. Except I don't think my arm moved. "I'm so tired."

"Joey! No. You need to stay awake, honey. Caphy's there with you?"

"Yeah. But LaLee's lost." Alarm shoved the shadows away for a beat. Panic sent the stars away. "We have to find her. She's in dang..."

"Joey? Joey!?"

"Coyotes will get her," I slurred.

"She's safe, honey. She came home. That's how I

knew you were lost. Can you stay awake for me, honey? I need you to call out when you hear me coming. Can you do that?"

I started to nod, but somebody speared my skull with a sword. "Ah!"

"Joey, can you stay awake for me?"

"Yep," I said, licking my dry lips again.

And then the charcoal slid completely over me. And the world sifted away.

I t was night. My eyes were closed, but I could feel darkness crawling around me. The sound of crickets was a soothing serenade against an unformed feeling of danger.

There was growling. Low and filled with unease. I felt it against my hip as I fought to regain consciousness.

A yip burst through the night, followed by another and another until a terrifying chorus of feral cries filled the darkness.

Caphy's growl deepened. She stood up and positioned herself above me, her trembling, muscular body hovering protectively.

She was scared. Caphy hardly ever got scared. I had to help her.

I shoved the blanket of fuzziness away and opened my eyes.

It was dark. Really dark. "What is it, girl?"

She shifted, whimpering softly, and returned her focus to the predators hiding in the dark. I'd heard the song of the coyotes before. It always gave me chills. Their music was a call to attend, a celebration of prey run to ground, and a chilling promise of impending death.

I shivered at the thought and shoved myself into a sitting position. Caphy didn't even look at me as I wrapped my arms around her trembling body. She was straddling my legs, vibrating.

Tears burned my eyes. "It'll be okay, sweet girl," I told her. Even though I was pretty sure it wouldn't.

Coyotes weren't known for attacking humans. But Caphy would fight to the death to protect me. And in the end, if they thought I was a danger to them, the predators would take me down too.

We were in trouble, and I needed to get off the ground and do something about it. I gritted my teeth against the pain in my head and pushed to my feet. Grabbing a thick branch that had been lying next to me, I held it as a barrier between us and our invisible stalkers. "Come on, girl. Let's go home."

Caphy's growl turned into a snarl and she bounced forward, teeth bared and a ferocious sound emerging from her chest.

The shadows shifted and several shapes oozed closer. The predators were perfectly, blood-chillingly silent. Unbelievably, that silence was worse than their feral calls had been.

More shadows shifted, spilling more predators into view.

Fear was a sour taste on the back of my tongue. "Crap," I muttered. I reached slowly toward Caphy, wrapping my fingers around her collar.

One of the coyotes moved toward us, its head down and its posture menacing...aggressive.

Spittle flew from Caphy's mouth as she snarled and lunged, nearly ripping me off my unsteady feet.

"No, Caphy," I said softly. "Come on." I started to back toward the ravine, tugging her with me. I had no idea what we'd do once we hit the incline, but I was crystal clear on what would happen if we stayed where we were.

Plans formed in my brain as we shuffled slowly backward. I'd keep Caphy close and get down the steep ravine wall any way we could. Even if we had to slide most of the way down. Once we found the bottom, I was praying the narrow, debris-clogged bottom would give us an advantage.

But I had no idea how we'd get back up the ravine with the predators moving in. I wasn't fast enough to outrun them. *One thing at a time*, I scolded myself.

I wanted to close my eyes against the throbbing pain in my head but didn't dare.

The coyotes moved stealthily forward, following

us as we backed away. My heel hit the edge of the gully and I stopped. Fear was a snake writhing through my chest. Once I started the decline we were going to be so vulnerable. I couldn't make myself take that next step.

Several feral gazes lit the night in front of me as if someone had flipped the *On* switch, setting them alight. I gasped. It was a nightmare-inducing sight. The glowing eyes lifted. The shadowy shapes behind them stilled.

Light slid over the ground on the other side of the ravine.

A flashlight!

"Joey!" Hal's worried voice was music to my ears...better than the finest angelic choir.

The predators halted, their eerie gazes sliding past us, to the spot where light flared in a barrier to the dark.

I held my breath as the coyotes hesitated. The biggest predator cast its gaze our way as if assessing whether it had time to get to us. I was afraid to call out, fearing it would spur the coyotes into attacking.

My head pounded, the rhythm matching the terrified beating of my heart.

I felt dizzy from the fear.

Finally, one of them turned away and melted into the night. One by one, the other coyotes followed its lead. Until only one remained. The biggest coyote locked its feral gaze on my snarling dog.

We were out of time.

"Here!" I screamed, never removing my gaze from the hungry predator. "We're here!" Tears slid down my cheeks as the last coyote finally gave up and melted away.

I sagged but kept my gaze riveted to the spot where they'd been. "We're here, Hal," I called again. And then I let a sob of pure relief escape.

7

"I'm fine," I insisted as Hal handed me a hot cup of tea and tucked the blankets around my legs.

"You're not fine," he said calmly. "You have a concussion."

I held my thumb and pointer finger a fraction of an inch apart. "Just a little one."

He didn't return my grin, his gaze sliding to the colorful bruise on the side of my face.

Feeling self-conscious about it, I tugged my hair over the multi-hued flesh.

"The doctor only let you come home because you promised to rest."

I made a face. The whole visit to the hospital the night before was kind of a blur. Except for the tantrum I threw when they tried to make me stay there. I remembered that clearly.

Despite my reluctance to stay in a hospital bed

overnight, being poked and prodded to ensure I never got any rest at all, it had been a relief when the ER doc had given me the good drugs to combat my raging headache. Vivid remnants of the pain still lived in my head, but it was much better than it had been. Fortunately, the gash at my hairline hadn't needed stitches, so there was only a mild concussion to deal with. The doc had finally agreed to let me go when Hal promised to stay close to check on me throughout the night. He'd had to leave his brother unattended for most of the night, but he'd assured me he'd checked in on Asher several times through the night and the kid was laying low at his cabin.

Looking into my PI's weary green gaze, guilt ate at me. I reached out and slid my fingers through his. "Thanks for babysitting me. Did you get any sleep at all?"

He kissed the back of my hand. "Enough. I'm going back to the spot where you were attacked to search for anything Arno can use to find the guy. I'm taking Caphy with me if you don't mind. We'll only be gone a couple of hours at most."

I slid a resentful look toward the pibl. "Traitor," I told her. She grinned back, her muscular tail beating a jaunty rhythm against the floor.

"Do you want me to call Lis to keep you company?"

"Not on your life. She has a showing today. The Thompson house will make her commission for the year if she can close it." The massive house sat on a bluff high above the Fawn River and boasted some of the best views of any home in the area. It was also worth just over a million dollars. Lis's boss, Madge Watson, had been trying to get the Thompson's to put the house on the market since she'd opened the office in Deer Hollow a couple of years earlier. Lis had not only managed to talk the elderly couple into selling, but she appeared to be one showing away from selling it.

With that one sale, Lis would seal her value and prove herself a worthy addition to Deer Hollow Realty. No way was I going to get in the way of all that. Not for a little headache.

Okay, maybe it was slightly more than a little headache. I was pretty sure the marching band had added a bass section since I'd woken up in the woods.

Hal leaned down and kissed my forehead. "Keep the doors locked. You have your phone?"

I held my cell up for him to see.

He nodded. "Call Asher if you need help with anything. He has the 4-wheeler, so he can be here in twenty minutes."

I sighed. "I'll be fine. How much trouble can I get into lying on this stupid couch."

"Famous last words," Hal muttered.

He slid a glance at LaLee. The cat was stretched along the back of the couch, watching him as if he were an untrustworthy rodent invader. Her expression said she would put up with him as long as he didn't irritate her delicate feline sensibilities. But if he stepped out of line, the cat would be just as happy to eat him.

As if reading my mind, LaLee licked her lips.

"Keep an eye on her," Hal said to the cat.

"Yowl!" *Don't tell me what to do, stupid human.*

I hid a grin. As soon as Hal and Caphy left, I shoved the covers off my legs and rose, jerking to a halt as my brain rolled painfully around inside my skull. "Ugh!" I said, holding my head as if to keep everything inside. "That hurts."

"Meow!" LaLee scolded.

"I know, but I have stuff to do."

"Meow?"

"Well, for starters, I need a shower in the worst way."

"Meow," she agreed. I sighed, lowering myself gently back to the couch. "I'll just take a little nap and then have my shower."

LaLee jumped onto the cushion and draped herself over my chest as if to hold me down. Soothing vibrations filled my chest as she started to purr.

Even if I'd wanted to get up, it wasn't going to happen. Not until my attack cat slash enforcer nanny decided I could.

Despite the pain in my brain, I slept deeply. Even the dreams that had kept me restless the night before gave way under the pain pills and tea Hal had practically forced down my throat. I probably would have slept another couple of hours if there hadn't been a disturbance in the force. A.k.a. my enforcer nanny.

"Yowl! Hsssss!"

The angry sound broke through my sleep. My eyes popped open as LaLee leaped to her feet, her long tail whipping me across the face.

At first, I saw nothing but the angry cat's butt. "LaLee, what's the deal?" I pushed myself higher on the pillow and jerked to a stop, my eyes going wide and my heart pounding a rapid beat beneath my ribs.

All the air exploded from my lungs.

The man leaning against the wall in my line of sight was extremely good looking. He was a couple of inches over six feet, with mahogany-brown hair that was thick and wavy. He wore it tucked behind his ears and curling softly at the back of his muscular neck. The man crossed his arms over his broad chest and settled a piercing charcoal-gray gaze on me. "Hello, Joey."

LaLee hissed again at the sound of his voice, her lean form going rigid with outrage.

I didn't bother grabbing hold of her. If she felt like taking a bite out of him as she had the last time he'd shown up at my house uninvited, I fully supported the idea. "How did you get into my house?"

His smile was smug. "You really should get better locks," he told me, glancing around my living room. "And a security system."

"I have a security system. Her name is Caphy."

Garland Medford lifted his hands and looked around, brow lowered as if confused. "And yet, she's not here."

I pressed my lips together. "What do you want, Medford?"

He stared at me a moment, an unidentifiable emotion skittering through his dark gaze. "Who hurt you?"

Heat filled my cheeks and, before I could stop myself, I reached up and tugged my blonde hair over the bruise. "Nobody. I fell." Not entirely a lie. I did fall. Right before somebody clocked me on the head.

Doubt flashed through the piercing charcoal gaze. "You don't need to be afraid of me," he said. "I thought I made that clear the last time we met."

Oh, I remembered. It was when he'd shown up at an abandoned home near the river and killed the woman who'd been holding me hostage. He'd also taken the money my hostage-taker had stolen from another thief.

To say that my relationship with the man who'd invaded my rest and my home was knotty would be the understatement of the century.

"The only thing you proved the last time is that you're ruthless, and you're a thief."

"That's a fair point from your perspective. But I did tell you there were things you didn't understand." He frowned, moving away from the wall to sit in a chair closer to me.

Growling a warning, LaLee stayed perched on my belly, every hair on her body lifted in outrage. I considered moving her so I could sit up. I felt at a disadvantage lying on the couch while Medford sat. But something told me not to make any sudden moves.

Medford was too much like the predators Caphy and I had faced the night before.

I shuddered at the thought.

"Are you cold?" Medford asked.

"Don't worry about that. Why are you in my house?" I asked again.

He sighed, sitting back and crossing one long leg over the other. His ankles were bare above the expensive loafers he seemed to prefer. I pegged him to be in his mid to late forties, but even so, the man was seriously gorgeous, and he knew it. "I warned you before that there were things you didn't know. Dangerous things. I've come to warn you that you're about to bump up against one of those things." He leaned forward, resting his tanned forearms on his knees. Medford was wearing dark wash jeans with a golf shirt in cotton candy pink that looked really good with his gray eyes and tanned skin. He seemed as comfortable in the jeans as he always had in his expensive suits. His brows lowered and he pursed his lips. "From the looks of your face, it appears I might already be too late with my warning." Seeing my disbelieving expression, he sighed. "I'm concerned," he said, clearly not comfortable with the admission.

"You're concerned?" I laughed. "That's rich."

What was the man up to? I had no doubt he was playing some kind of game.

The wealthy businessman, slash uber-criminal, shook his head. "I know you don't believe this, but I don't want to see you or anyone you care about get hurt."

"Is that a threat?"

He shook his head. I wasn't sure if it was in denial of my accusation, or a sign of his frustration. "You know what I'm involved in…"

"Yes." If all the rumors were true, he dabbled in drugs, prostitution, and murder for hire. Not that he personally poked his well-manicured fingers into those very ugly pies. He was just the force behind the force, so to speak.

"There's a man. His name is unimportant. But he's been trying to build a name for himself in the drug organizations of Indianapolis and Chicago. He's doing that by using children to sell the drugs." Medford stared at me, no doubt seeing the surprise in my eyes. "Yes. Your Mr. Amity's brother is in more trouble than you believed. This man I'm talking about. He'll kill the boy if he believes he's a loose end."

All the blood ran from my face. "Are you doing anything to stop him?"

"It's complicated." He grimaced as if his answer didn't make him any happier than it made me. Medford stood. "You needed to know. But..." his face tightened. "You mustn't tell Amity you got that information from me."

I shook my head. "I have to tell him."

Medford shoved his hands into the pockets of his pristine jeans. "I took a great risk coming here to warn you, Joey." His gaze held a pleading note I never thought I'd see from the arrogant, powerful man. "I'm asking you not to give me away."

"Why?"

"There are people who would take a dim view of my interference. Those people hold the key to a lot of things, and my being here would risk throwing a wrench into those things." He shook his head. "I can't tell you what you want to know. It's become the story of my life." Medford gave me a smile that didn't quite reach his eyes. "You take care, Joey."

And then he was gone.

I climbed to my feet as the front door closed. Ignoring the waves of knife-like pain slicing through my head, I hurried to the front door. By the time I'd thrown it open, Medford had disappeared. There was no car driving away. He wasn't walking across my yard. I hurried out and descended to the driveway, looking up into the painful brightness of a clear day. No helicopter cut a path through the cloudless sky.

Medford had simply disappeared. Like a ghost. Again.

B y the time Hal and Caphy returned, I was in the kitchen fixing grilled cheese sandwiches and tomato soup. LaLee was perched on a tall stool at the island, cleaning her dainty paws after the snack of cheddar cheese I'd given her.

I counted my blessings that she wasn't sitting on the island.

Hal looked surprised to see me standing at the stove. I turned and gave him a smile. "Hey. Did you find anything?"

Hal narrowed his gaze. "What are you doing on your feet?"

I slid my spatula under a perfectly browned

sandwich, transferring it to a plate. "Making your favorite lunch."

He continued to look slightly suspicious as he scanned a look over me. "You showered and changed."

I handed him the plate and bowl of soup because, if I'd put them on the island, the cat would have carted the sandwich away before I could yell her name. "I did. I feel so much better."

He relented finally, softening his gaze. "I'm glad. Do you want tea? Or lemonade?"

"Lemonade, please."

We busied ourselves with the domesticity of lunch for a few minutes and then sat together at the little table in front of the window that overlooked my back yard. I sipped the icy lemonade and sighed. "That's good."

Caphy dropped her big head on my thigh and looked up at me with pleading eyes. I gave her a look. "I don't know. You ran off without me this morning. You didn't even look back."

She whined pitifully.

Grinning, Hal said, "If it makes you feel better, she kept stopping and whining at me until the house was out of sight."

I rolled my eyes. "For a full five minutes, huh?" I finally relented, giving her a piece of my crust with cheese melted on the edges. "You didn't answer my question," I nudged. "Did you find anything?"

Hal nodded, wiping his lips with a paper napkin. "I found the branch he hit you with." Hal grimaced. "There's blood on it."

My pulse rose at the memory of being struck and the horrific helplessness of being surrounded by the coyotes. "Can they get fingerprints off of it?" I was only half joking. I watched a lot of CSI shows and knew that, at least on TV, such things were sometimes possible.

"Doubtful. But Arno might be able to do something with this." He tapped his cell phone and then offered it to me. The picture he'd queued up looked like nothing but well-churned mud with some sticks and a few chunks of torn leaves. "What am I looking at?"

"It's easier to see in person. It's a footprint. Arno might be able to run it through their evidence database and identify the tread. I've never seen that particular tread before. Hopefully, it's unique enough to identify a pool of possible suspects."

That sounded like a long way to go for little result. As I'd been doing since Medford left, I struggled to come up with a possible way to tell Hal about the drug king in Indianapolis without telling him about Medford's visit.

In addition to worrying about coming up with a plausible way to warn Hal, I was dealing with guilt over what would amount to lying. I'd made it a practice never to lie to Hal. The one time he'd lied to me by omission, it had been about something relatively trivial. His moving into the house my Uncle Devon had once lived in on the adjoining property. But I'd been really mad at him about the lie. So much so that I felt like a hypocrite even considering lying to him about what Medford had told me.

My mind in a whirl, I ate in silence.

Hal's warm hand covered mine after a few minutes. "Are you still mad that we left you behind?"

"Huh? Oh. Not at all. I get it. I tried to get off the couch after you left, and I'm pretty sure my brain nearly slid out my ears."

Hal laughed. "Stubborn woman."

I shrugged. "Yeah, but you wouldn't have me any other way, right?"

"Well..." Hal's eyes sparkled.

I shook my head. "I guess I'm just still tired."

Hal took my plate and bowl. "I'll clean up. Why don't you go lie down for a while? I brought my laptop. I'll get some work done while you rest."

I nodded. "Thanks." Halfway to the door, I stopped. "Has Arno gotten any more information about the girl in Indy?"

Hal started rinsing plates. "No."

I hesitated. "Could the person who's giving Ash's friend the drugs to sell come after him here?"

Hal stilled, turning to give me a surprised look. "Where did that come from?"

I tried to look innocent, but that wasn't my best thing. "Just a thought."

"You think the organization behind those drugs was in your woods last night and attacked you?" He seemed so astounded by my suggestion, I felt silly for offering it. Even though I knew why I had.

"You're right, that's crazy. It just seems like a big coincidence. Anyway..." I scurried out of there fast. But not fast enough that I didn't feel Hal's speculative gaze burning the skin of my back as I left.

8

"You were right about the tracks," Arno told Hal. The cell was on speaker, and I listened as Hal and I sat in the porch swing and watched the animals play in the yard. Caphy was smacking the muddy water at the edge of the pond, jumping with alarm every time the water hit her between the eyes in retaliation. A few yards away from the pibl, LaLee leaped straight into the air and smacked at a butterfly that managed to evade her killer paws. She landed hard, tail whipping as if shocked at having failed in her assault. Ethel Squeaks was digging up dandelions in the front yard. She had a special fondness for the tender roots of the weeds and I was happy to let her rid the yard of them.

Hal and I were enjoying a multi-colored pre-sunset sky, talking about heading into town later for dinner at Sonny's and maybe a movie.

Asher had gone to a party in town with Ame, so we had a free night ahead of us that I was really looking forward to filling with low-stress fun.

"You identified the type of shoe?" Hal asked, perking up.

"The tread is from a special kind of high-top sneaker that's popular with the post-high-school crowd."

Hope died from Hal's gaze. "So, the suspect pool is everyone over eighteen?"

"Eighteen to twenty-three-ish," Arno said. There was a tinge of humor in his voice. "But not really. I talked to a store in Indy that sells them. The clerk said the shoes are five hundred dollars a pair."

Hal whistled. "Are they made of gold?"

"Might as well be. They're handmade. The spokesperson for the shoes was a famous basketball star who died young in a helicopter crash."

"Ah. So there's star power and sentiment behind them," Hal said, nodding. Got it. "Do you have a list of all the buyers?"

"Not a comprehensive one. Five stores sell the shoes in Indy. But we need to consider our perp could have bought them in Chicago. They're also sold in limited stores in Nashville and Cincinnati."

Hal gave me a bleak look. "Have you run the Indianapolis buyer's list for persons connected to the case?"

"We've got twenty-five buyers since January. So

far, nobody we're looking at for this *particular* case is on the list."

I heard the inflection in his statement. "This particular case?" I asked. "Is there someone we haven't included that we would recognize?"

Arno hesitated a beat, and my pulse picked up. I suddenly knew what he was going to say. "Yeah. I'm afraid an old friend of yours is on the list, Joey."

I closed my eyes. "Garland Medford."

Hal skimmed me a surprised look.

"Got it in one," Arno said.

"Isn't he a little old for this type of shoe?" Hal asked. His gaze never left mine. It was filled with questions I couldn't answer.

Feeling guilty, I avoided the unspoken questions by avoiding his gaze.

"Yeah. It makes you wonder who he bought them for."

Yeah, I thought. *It certainly does.* "We need to find out if Asher's friends have those shoes," I said. "What do they look like?"

Arno didn't answer my question. Instead, he said, "Joey, you need to stay out of this."

"This person attacked me on my own property, Arno," I told him, anger making the residual ache in my head pound harder. "I have a right to get involved."

Hal clasped my hand and gave it a squeeze.

"She's right, Arno. Joey was attacked. Someone has targeted her, and we need to find out why."

"I'm sure she was just in the wrong place at the wrong time," Arno said. Unfortunately for him, his voice didn't hold the conviction it needed to convince us to let it go.

"On my own property?" I said. At my slightly shrill tone, I cleared my throat. "What possible reason would someone have to attack me on my property?"

"Maybe they were trespassing." Arno offered. "Maybe they were doing something they didn't want to get in trouble for." He hesitated. "Besides the shoe tracks, what else did you find in the area, Amity?"

"No evidence of drugs. No 4-wheeler tracks. Nothing to suggest a struggle beyond the spot where Joey was attacked. All I found was the branch Joey was struck with and those prints in the dirt."

"Can you tell me what you remember, Joey?" Arno asked. I'd given my statement to Hal when he found me in the woods, and then again over the phone to Arno when my head was clearer. But, I understood that sometimes details emerged after enough time had passed. "Caphy, LaLee, and I were taking a walk. Caphy got too far ahead of me, and I thought I saw a coyote, so I panicked."

"What exactly did you see? Are you sure it was a coyote?"

My instinct was to just say yes. After all, I'd definitely seen coyotes when I'd woken up later. But I hadn't actually gotten a good look. "All I know for sure is that I saw something moving through the trees on the other side of the ravine. It was low to the ground like a dog or a coyote."

"But it could have been someone bent low and running?"

I didn't think so, but it was possible. That's what I told him.

"Okay, go on."

"LaLee took off after Caphy, and I was right behind her. It took me longer to scale the ravine and when I got to the top, I couldn't see my dog. She was barking with a high-pitched sound that meant she'd cornered something. I panicked and started to run. But I tripped."

"Wait," Arno said, interrupting. "You tripped? What did you trip on?"

"Yeah, I told you I tripped, right?" I looked at Hal, but he shook his head. "Sorry, yeah, I think my sneaker got caught in a root. It happens all the time in those woods. The roots are everywhere."

"Okay, you tripped," Arno said in a soft, leading type of voice. "Is it possible you just hit your head on that branch when you fell? Are you sure someone hit you with it?"

Pain sliced across my forehead and my thoughts dulled, becoming tangled. I rubbed at the pain, trying to wipe it away.

"Honey?" Hal rubbed a big, warm hand over my back. "Are you okay?"

I nodded. "Fine. I'm just trying to remember every detail."

"Take your time, Joey," Arno said. "I want you to remember it right. There's no pressure."

Except that there *was* pressure. I'd already forgotten to give them one important detail. Heaven knew what else I'd missed.

I closed my eyes and pulled the memory forward. Impressions eased into view, playing across my mind like a bad horror film.

Fear making it hard to breathe. My fingers aching from the rough climb to the top of the ravine. My knees burning. I'd scraped them on a big rock that was mostly buried in the mud when I fell. I'd been panting, skimming my gaze through the quickly darkening woods. LaLee was ahead of me. LaLee disappeared under that big evergreen, its heavy branches dipping low to the ground.

I'd picked myself up off the ground, started forward.

A shape appeared out of nowhere, just on the edge of my peripheral vision. Agony burst on the side of my head. I slammed downward.

"Yes," I told Arno, opening my eyes. "Someone hit me. I'm sure of it."

"Can you give me a description? Anything at all?"

"No. Sorry. I barely saw them, and it happened too fast."

"Okay. I'll keep working the shoes and let you know what I find."

"Joey and I will check the local hotels to see if anybody new has checked in over the last few days."

"Okay," Arno agreed.

Hal held my gaze as he added, "Then I'd like to visit with Will Zola and Kevin Rich. I'll approach them as Asher's brother. Maybe they'll tell me more than they would a cop."

Arno was silent for a beat, thinking about it. "You'd have to make it clear that you're not there as a representative of any police organization."

"Understood."

"Okay, you're right. They might talk to you. Touch base when you get back into town and let me know what you find out?"

"Will do. Thanks, Arno. Will you send me a picture of the shoes we're looking for? Or a link to find them online?"

"Yep."

Hal disconnected and looked at me. "Feel like a trip into Indy?"

I grinned, relieved he was including me. "I thought you'd never ask."

O n the Southside of town, the Deer Hollow Motel...such a creative name... was a bust. As was the Blue Buck Inn North of Deer Hollow. Nobody new had checked into the hotels for over a week. Unless my attacker had been hanging around Deer Hollow for a lot longer than made sense, he hadn't stayed at either of them.

Hal pulled into The Fawn Hotel and parked. We sat for a moment, staring at the roiling waters of the Fawn River in the distance. Edged on the East by a steep, rocky cliff, the river cut a winding path through the untamed countryside and continued southward toward Kentucky. It was beautiful and wild, and its cliffs were prime real estate for the huge coyote population in the area.

My gaze sliding to the dark pocks in the cliffside that I knew were coyote dens, I shuddered in memory of my encounter with them.

"You okay?" Hal asked.

I gave him a slightly forced smile. "Fine. The river is looking a little wild today."

Nodding, Hal climbed out of the Escalade and walked around to open my door. He offered me his hand and tugged me gently free of the car, pulling me into a hug. His tall form felt solid and comforting as he gave me a lingering kiss.

My toes curled and heat coiled in my belly.

When he broke the kiss, he gave me a smile. "Let's eat dinner in Indy after talking to the boys."

The idea made me smile. "Great idea." Then I frowned. "We need to get someone to take care of the animals."

"You're right. Lis?"

"I'll call her."

"I'll go talk to the desk clerk while you make that call," Hal offered.

I nodded, quickly dialing. It rang several times before Lis picked up. "Hey, girl."

"Hey. Did you sell that house?"

"Not yet," my BFF responded with a smile in her voice. "But I'm close."

"Chicken dance!" I said, laughing. "I was wondering if you could do me a favor."

"Anything."

"Hal and I are heading to Indianapolis to question a couple of kids on this thing Asher's mixed up in. I was wondering if you could come over later and let the beasts out for a pee."

"Of course. Just Caphy and Ms. Squeaks?"

"Yeah. LaLee's good with her litter box. Besides, she might take off if you let her out."

"Got it. What time?"

"Around nine?"

"I can do that."

"Sorry to cut into date night," I told her, watching as Hal exited the building holding a key.

"You didn't. Arno got called in anyway. Listen, I have to go. Talk to you soon."

"Thanks, Lis!" I disconnected and looked at Hal. "You found something?"

"Manager says a guy stayed in one of the units for two nights. Checked out late last night. Paid cash."

I frowned. "So no paper trail."

"Right. And the guy wore a hoodie with a cap so no distinguishing characteristics. But let's go see if he left behind some other kind of trail."

The room was on the second floor of the long building. Access to all the rooms was from the exterior, like a motel, and I knew from the brochures the hotel spread around town that every room had a nice view of the river behind it. The stairs and balcony to the second level wore a fresh coat of bright white paint, a nice contrast to the sage green the main building had recently been painted. The windows along the front were small, set evenly between each door and the next room.

The Fawn billed itself as clean, cozy, and moderately priced. A step above the other lodgings in the area. From what I'd seen so far, they'd lived up to the marketing hype.

The doors were all painted navy blue. They and the windows looked brand new.

"Somebody's put some money into this place," I said. I vaguely remembered when the hotel had been purchased from its previous owners. If memory served, the person who'd bought it had been a wealthy businessman from Indy.

Hal opened the door of room 210 and stepped inside, his intense gaze skimming the main room and slowing at the door to the bathroom on the back wall. On the same wall as the bathroom, a picture window looked out over the picturesque river and the rocky terrain it wound through. A second door next to the window led to a small balcony that contained two chairs and a small table, set back so as not to impede the view of the river beyond.

"Nice."

Hal moved into the room and headed straight for the bathroom. I heard the sound of drawers and doors opening and closing, the squeal of a shower curtain being drawn back on a rod, and the unmistakable sound of a toilet lid being removed and replaced.

He came out empty-handed a few minutes later.

I stopped rifling through the drawers to grin at him. "The toilet? Really?"

Hal's dark green gaze twinkled. "It might sound strange, but believe it or not, bad guys think it's a creative spot to hide stuff."

I shook my head. "I'd rather go to prison than hide something I had to touch again in the toilet."

Hal chuckled. "Did you find anything?"

"Nothing in the dressers except a list of local restaurant and entertainment options."

"I'll bet that was short," Hal said.

I smacked him on the arm. "Watch it, buster."

He tugged the covers off the bed and searched around the base, even pulling the mattress up and turning it over.

Nothing.

I opened the closet and searched the shelves inside while Hal remade the bed. The hangers were empty, and the shelves held only extra pillows and an iron. The ironing board hung tidily on the back wall of the space. I was about to close the door when I spotted something on the floor. "Hal?"

He came up behind me. "Find something?"

"Will you turn on the overhead light there?" I jerked my chin toward the recessed light above our heads.

A moment later, the light came on and I saw exactly what I thought I'd seen. I pointed toward the floor. "Good thing the maid cut a corner," I told Hal, stepping back to let Hal take a closer look.

He knelt before the closet and used the light on his cell phone to better illuminate the muddy footprint on the carpet. "Got ya," Hal murmured, snapping some pictures of the print.

His cell rang as he was getting ready to call Arno. He glanced at the name on the screen, hitting *Accept* with a smile. "I was just going to call you," he told

Arno. He listened for a beat, the smile melting from his face. "Where?"

I frowned a question at him.

Hal didn't respond. "We'll be there in ten minutes." He disconnected and grabbed my arm. "Come on, we need to get to town."

I let him pull me into a run and followed him down the stairs. His expression was dire and ice formed along my spine. Something bad had happened. "What's wrong, Hal?" Then I had a terrible thought. "Is Asher okay?"

Hal jumped into his car and started it before I managed to climb into the passenger seat. He backed quickly, the Escalade's big tires kicking up gravel as he shot out of the lot. Hal stared straight ahead, his gaze locked on the road and his jaw tight.

"You're scaring me," I told him. "What's going on?"

He risked a quick glance in my direction. The fear in his eyes was almost my undoing. "It's Asher."

I gasped, my hand finding his muscular forearm as I leaned close. "Is he hurt?"

"Not yet," Hal said. "But if I get my hands on him, he will be."

9

Three Sheriff's Deputy cars were arrayed across the residential street when we pulled up. Their lights flashed through the night, painting the trees and homes in blue and red lights. The ambulance was waiting with lights flaring against the darkness, and a cluster of worried-looking kids stood close together up near the house.

My gaze slid to the small, slender form draped between a tidy bed of bushes at the corner of the residential lot. A vibrant array of delicate flowers lay crushed beneath her twisted form.

The girl was petite, her dark hair spread across her unnaturally pale face, and her fingers formed into claws, the tips buried in the black mulch beneath her. Her blue eyes were clouded and blank, death having already staked a claim on them.

One slender leg, clad in black leggings, was stretched straight, toes rigidly pointing. Her hips were twisted and her other leg was bent across the first, as if she'd been writhing in pain.

A single, slender pump lay inches away from her pale foot, the other clung to the toes of her outstretched leg.

She was utterly still.

Arno was standing beside his cruiser, head down as he spoke to someone I couldn't see.

Hal called out as we hurried over and Arno moved to the side, revealing Asher.

The kid's face was chalky, his eyes deep pools of fear as the lights of the radio cars strobed over him. His hands were behind his back, and it didn't take a genius to know he'd been cuffed.

"Oh no, Hal," I said.

Hal pulled air into his lungs and took my hand, squeezing it like a lifeline as we approached the two men. "Is he under arrest?" Hal asked Arno.

Arno's gaze was hard, angry, and when he looked at Hal, it wasn't the look of a friend to another friend. "He's a person of interest," Arno said. "I'm taking him in and keeping him overnight."

Hal's body turned to rock against me. "Are the cuffs really necessary?"

Arno's jaw tightened. He lifted his right hand and showed us a small, clear bag with red Evidence tape across the top. "These were in his pocket when I searched him."

Hal looked at the pills in the bag, and a small sound escaped him. It was like the sound of a wounded animal. "Asher?"

The kid's eyes were dark pools against the chalk of his face. He was shaking his head. "Those aren't mine. I don't know how they got in my pocket. I swear."

"Says every drug dealer ever," Arno muttered, looking disgusted.

"He's not lying," said a shrill voice behind us. We turned to see Ame, looking nearly as white as Asher. "He didn't give Rhonda Mae any pills. He never even spoke to her."

The girl's face was wet, her beautiful eyes puffy from crying. I opened my arm and she came into it, sobbing against my shoulder. "He didn't kill her," Ame said softly. "He was with me the whole time."

Hal flinched at her words, a muscle in his jaw jumping. "Ash, don't say anything else until I can get you a lawyer."

Arno settled an angry look on Hal but finally nodded. "That's good advice." He jerked his head at a deputy standing nearby. I recognized the diminutive cop as Deputy Mark Sheppard. Sheppard had once been assigned to help Hal and me with a case. He was both the most annoying person I'd ever met and the most dedicated. The deputy glanced my way, an apology clear in his gaze, and took Asher's arm, easing him into the cruiser's back seat.

We watched the car drive away a moment later, and Hal turned on Arno. "You don't actually believe my brother killed that girl, do you?"

Arno scrubbed a hand over his face, cutting the distance between them in half and lowering his voice. "It's not what I believe, Amity. It's where the evidence takes me."

"Your evidence is garbage," Hal growled out.

His jaw tight, Arno nodded, looking at his shoes. "Well, then find me some that isn't garbage," he said. He lifted his gaze to lock on Hal's, the message clear. He didn't want to arrest Asher for the teenaged girl's death, but he'd do what he had to do.

"I want to question the witnesses," Hal barked, clearly not willing to be appeased.

"You know I can't let you do that," Arno said. "You need to stay as far away from this investigation as possible."

"That's not going to happen," Hal told him. He turned on his heel and strode back toward the car. I looked at Arno. "You have to let him do something," I said, my voice pleading. "What can we do?"

He sighed. "Go to Indianapolis and talk to those boys. I'm not going to press charges on Asher until I have to. I'll hold him as long as I can."

I nodded. "Thanks, Arno."

"Just try to keep your boyfriend calm." He started

to turn away and then turned back, his expression filled with understanding. "I get it. Believe me. When I had to arrest my mom..." He scrubbed his face with both hands. "Amity was a godsend. I'll return the favor on this, Joey. But if it starts to look as if the kid's guilty?" He shrugged.

I nodded my understanding and hurried to the car. Hal paced alongside the Escalade like a trapped animal. "Arno wants us to go talk to those boys."

He expelled air. "Good." He opened the car door for me. "I need to find Ash a lawyer. Who do you have around here that can keep him out of trouble?"

I grimaced.

His eyes went wide. "Not a chance."

I shrugged. "He's the only local lawyer we have. We can maybe find someone in Indianapolis, but it's seven o'clock. If you want someone at the jail tonight, it'll have to be him."

Hal clearly didn't like it, but he knew I was right. "I'm definitely going to regret this," he told me, firmly closing my door.

"I already do," I murmured as he hurried around the car.

George Shulz's office resided in a small clapboard house located on a short road that branched off Main Street in Deer Hollow. A large, gold and black sign in the yard proclaimed it the *Shulz Law Practice*, with George Shulz's name and letters spelled out in six-inch-high letters.

The house and the sign both appeared to be even more droopy than the last time we'd followed the brick sidewalk to the front door. It was as if the whole thing was built above the pits of Hell, and Satan was slowly reclaiming it.

Having the extreme displeasure of having met Shulz a few times, I could fully believe he was one of Satan's demons being called home. He'd once told me that around sixty percent of his clients threatened to kill him after spending any time with him. A smaller percentage tried to have him committed. As a self-described sociopath, Shulz wasn't anybody's idea of a good time. He likely only survived professionally because he had no competition in the area.

Pale light shone behind the windows of Shulz's house, telling us he was probably home. I hoped that meant he'd be willing to take on being Asher's legal bulwark for us. Hal reached for the front door and stopped, seeming to brace himself against what was coming.

I shared his dread. Shulz was beyond horrible as

a human being, and his office could aptly be named a true pit of despair. But despite his shortcomings, I suspected the man was a decent enough lawyer. If just slightly unethical.

The door was unlocked and, as soon as we entered the building, Hal succumbed to a bout of violent sneezing.

Did I mention Shulz hoarded cats and Hal is violently allergic to feline type creatures? He generally took an antihistamine when he was going to be around LaLee, but the cat situation at Shulz's office went well beyond the scope of one little pill. I wasn't sure there were enough pills in the world to counteract the abundance of cat hair and dander in the little office.

The "office" portion of Shulz's home smelled like mildew, old books, and cat pee. If it weren't for all the cats lounging around, I'd think Shulz was running a meth lab.

He certainly looked the type.

The office consisted of three walls filled with a mismatched array of shelves that bulged with books, old and new. The wall opposite the entry held a door to a small bathroom, which probably grew unknown and deadly pathogens that were best not explored. Next to the door was a short counter with two cabinets, a sink, and a coffee maker. Piles of paper overlaid every free inch of the counter, likely the overflow from the piles covering the long farm table that dominated the room.

At the center of the long table, his greasy dark head barely visible above a pile of files and paper, George Shulz peered at us with a judgmental and slightly near-sighted gaze.

A fat orange cat lay across the pile of paper nearest the door, its tail unnaturally short and its green eyes narrowed with hostility. "Meow!"

I blew off the cat's hostility, having suffered more than my share of it from LaLee.

Poor Hal sneezed again.

Shulz's gaze narrowed with practiced disdain. "Peligrine and Loraine Foster. Four counts of Meth-amphetamine production and two counts of peddling said Meth to minors. Pew sitters extraordinaire and all-around horrible people who believe the laws are simply a minor inconvenience that is best ignored."

Shulz insisted on playing the client guessing game whenever we visited. I wasn't sure if it was just to irritate potential clients, or if he really didn't remember who was who on his client list. Either way, it was clear that client confidentiality was a low priority for the despicable man.

Hal shook his head. "Try again, Shulz."

The greasy head tilted. His eyes widened. "Ah, Jeffrey Tolbine, a glad-handing, would-be politician who throws his money around trying to buy his way out of trouble. I've personally gotten you off of six speeding tickets, four parking violations, and one charge of domestic terrorism..."

I felt my own eyes widen as I looked at Hal. "Domestic terrorism?"

Hal's lips quirked in a grin. "Just another day in the office."

I snorted out a laugh, earning me a narrowing of Shulz's dead eyes. "Polly Milford, aging cheerleader, charged with five counts of solicitation and one charge of public nudity..."

Hal arched a brow. "Why, Polly, you naughty girl."

I jammed my hands on my hips, glaring at Shulz. "Aging?"

The man stood and glared at us. "State your business or skedaddle. I have work to do."

Hal sneezed again as a small, gray cat sashayed past, rubbing enthusiastically against his jeans. "I need to hire you," he said quickly before sneezing again.

Shulz gave a put-upon sigh. "What is the nature of the charge?"

Hal scowled over the handkerchief he was using to contain a barrage of sneezes.

"His brother hasn't been charged yet," I told Shulz.

"We need you to represent him until I can get him cleared," Hal said, sniffling.

"Why is he being detained?"

Hal stuffed the hankie into his jeans pocket, looking miserable. "Possible negligent homicide and sale of an illegal substance."

Shulz suddenly became more interested. "I see. Well then, I'm your man." He dug through a teetering pile of paper and came up with a form, handing it to Hal. "Fill this out. My retainer is five hundred for tonight and three hundred a day thereafter."

I sucked air, but Hal didn't seem surprised by the amount. He took the pen Shulz handed him and dropped into a chair, carving out a small area on the table for the form.

Shulz and I stared at each other across the table. I briefly considered setting him straight on who I was, but the last time I'd been there, he'd taken great pleasure informing me that my parents were horrible people and implying my mother didn't love me enough to stick around.

I wasn't eager to reengage that particular conversation.

Shulz sneered at the bruise on my face. "One of your johns beat you up, Polly?" He grinned as if the idea of me taking a beating was hilarious.

I curled my lip at him, a growl vibrating in my throat.

When we were leaving twenty minutes later, Shulz said, "You know, Tolbine, if this..." he glanced down at the form... "Asher Amity is a friend of yours, it would be best if you removed all traces of fertilizer from his home before the police search it. I don't like my chances of getting him off for murder *and* domestic terrorism."

Hal didn't even bother to argue. He just ushered me through the door and to the car, inhaling great gulps of fresh air as he went.

We rode in silence for the three-quarters of an hour it took to reach Brown County. Hal was caught up in his thoughts, and I felt like I should give him the time to come to terms with Asher's predicament. I was eternally grateful to Arno for allowing Hal to interview Asher's friends. Hal would be going completely stir crazy if he couldn't help in some way.

Hal pulled off the highway near an outlet mall and headed into the countryside, toward a little town called Franklin.

"How do you know where Will Zola lives?" I asked my PI.

He turned left at a light and sped past a mix of nice homes and wide-open farmland. "I looked him and Kevin Rich up after I talked to Dad. He warned me they were in the middle of this mess with Asher and said those two were the reason Ash got into trouble."

"Do you believe that?"

Hal didn't answer right away. He seemed to be giving it some thought. Finally, he sighed. "I know my brother. He's had a bee in his knickers since he was old enough to create his own kind of chaos in the world. He likes to stretch boundaries, even when those boundaries happen to be laws. Will Zola and Kevin Rich are responsible for their own part in whatever went down. Asher's responsible for whatever part he played. I can't give him a pass. My only goal tonight is to find out what we're dealing with, and whether it's possible that it followed Ash to Deer Hollow."

I reached over and slid my fingers through his, giving his hand a squeeze. "I don't know your brother as well as you do, but for what it's worth, I think he's a good person."

Hal looked slightly bemused when he glanced my way. "Yeah? What exactly are you basing that on?"

I shrugged. "Simple. Caphy and Ethel Squeaks like him."

Hal chuckled. "Maybe, but LaLee hates him."

I let my lips curve in a smile. "I rest my case."

Will Zola bent over a motorcycle in the asphalt drive of his parents' upper-middle-class home. Bathed in the bright white light of the oversized carriage lights above each door, the bike gleamed a deep red as the kid rubbed it with a rag.

Will glanced our way as Hal pulled up the long drive and stopped, his face illuminated in the Escalade's headlights. He turned expectantly as Hal climbed out of the car, barely giving me a glance.

"Will Zola?"

Suspicion quickly gave way to recognition as the kid focused on Hal. He grinned, showing uneven white teeth. "You've got to be one of Asher's brothers."

Hal offered the kid his hand. "Hal Amity."

Will bobbed his head, his pale red curls dancing with the movement. The teen rubbed his freckled hands with the rag. "Is Ash okay? We haven't heard from him for a couple of days."

"He's been better. I understand that you, Kevin Rich, and Asher were mixed up in a suspicious death investigation."

The kid's smile slid away. "You don't waste time, do ya, man?"

"Asher's sitting in the Deer Hollow police station because another girl overdosed from drugs. I need to find out how the two deaths are connected."

Will bristled. "And you came to accuse me? I'm here, man. I don't know nothin' about no dead girl in hicksville." He threw the rag over the seat of his bike. "Asher's there. Ask him."

Nice, I thought. *Throw your friend to the wolves.* "Funny," I said, frowning. "Asher defended you and Kevin Rich. But you seem to be accusing him of killing someone. I guess his loyalty is misplaced, huh?"

The kid stared at me a beat. I saw the moment he realized he might still need Ash on his side. "It's not like that. I'm just sayin' I don't know anything about what's going on down there."

"What about the girl who died here?" Hal asked. "You know anything about that?"

Will shrugged. "Me and the guys went to school with her. She was kind of a party girl. Nobody was surprised when she O.D.'d."

"Where'd she get the drugs?" Hal asked the kid.

"No idea." He must have seen disbelief in Hal's expression. "I swear, man. Me and the boys don't get into that stuff. It's stupid. I've seen what happened to guys who mess with drugs. I want no part of that."

"What about Kevin Rich?" Hal asked.

"What about him?"

"Was he selling Oxy to the other kids?"

Will snorted. "Where we gonna get that stuff?" He shook his head. "Not a chance. I'm tellin' ya, man, you're barkin' up the wrong tree."

Hal nodded, hands shoved into the pockets of his jeans. "Nice bike."

Will turned with a smile. "Isn't she a beauty?"

"Is it new?"

"Just picked her up today." He caressed the leather seat, his freckled face aglow.

"Must have cost a lot," Hal said, his gaze fixed on Will.

The kid started to shrug and then stilled, his expression turning shrewd. "If you're done asking me questions, I should go inside."

"One more," Hal said, pulling out his cell and holding it up for the kid to see. "Do you own sneakers like this?"

Will shrugged. "Lots of people own those sneakers."

It was a non-answer that told me the kid probably had a pair of the shoes.

The front door opened and a tall man, slender to the point of emaciated and with bright red hair, came out onto the porch, his expression tight. "Can I help you with something?"

"Mr. Zola?"

"That's right." The man's gaze slid to me and then back to Hal. "Who are you?"

Hal strode over and offered the man his hand. Zola stepped down from the porch and took it. "Hal Amity."

"Asher's brother?"

Hal gave the man a smile. "One of them, yes."

Zola's narrow face folded into a frown. "Is Asher okay? We haven't heard from him since..." He slid his gaze to his son, his jaw tightening, and then back to Hal. "For a while."

"He's staying in Deer Hollow with me."

Mr. Zola stared at Hal. "Why are you here, Mr. Amity?"

"He was askin' me about selling drugs," Will said.

Will's father stiffened. He crossed his arms over his chest, the pale red hairs that covered his well-toned forearms glistening in the porch light. "You'll need to speak to my lawyer about that."

"I'm not here as a representative of the police," Hal said, his tone friendly. "I'm here because something's happened in Deer Hollow."

Zola cocked his head. "Something?"

"A girl died from what looks like an OxyContin overdose. Asher's being held as a person of interest. I thought, given what happened here, that the two deaths might be connected somehow."

Zola nodded. "I understand your concern, Mr. Amity..."

"Please, call me Hal."

"Hal..." Zola's smile was insincere. It was obvious he didn't like us being there. "But I'm afraid I can't have Will getting involved. He can't help it if some girl took too much of her own stash. The last thing he needs is to get dragged into another unfortunate death. I'm sorry."

Hal nodded, taking it much better than I'd expected. "Maybe you could just answer one question for me?"

Zola relaxed when he realized Hal wasn't going to press him. "I'll try."

"Do you have any ideas who might be selling these drugs to the kids?"

"That's the million-dollar question, isn't it?" Zola said, shaking his head. He scraped his foot, covered in an expensive-looking loafer, across the bricks of the sidewalk, seemingly trying to decide if he wanted to respond. Finally, he looked up at Hal, his pale gaze narrowing. "If you tell anyone I said this, I'll call you a liar."

Hal nodded. "Understood. This will remain between you and me."

I tried to shrink into the night so Zola wouldn't notice I'd be witnessing the secret as well.

He glanced toward the darkened street, his gaze scanning it as if looking for spies. Then he sighed. "When the boys initially got into trouble, I used my connections in Johnson County to find out who might be involved in this type of thing. One name kept coming back to me."

"Who was it?" Hal prompted.

"Garland Medford. Word on the street is that he's

got the organization, the connections, and the money to front this type of operation."

My stomach twisted, and I found myself leaning against the Escalade as my knees threatened to give out.

Was Medford responsible?

Had his visit to me been an attempt to get out ahead of what he knew was about to happen?

If so, had the girl been murdered? Or was it truly an accident?

"Joey?"

I blinked, realizing too late that Hal had been talking to me. I looked around and saw that Mr. Zola and Will had disappeared. "Sorry. I was just thinking."

Hal reached around me and opened my door, waiting until I slipped inside.

I watched him walk around the front of the car and slide into the driver's seat. "Where to now?"

"Home," Hal said, his expression dire.

I blinked in surprise. "We're not going to talk to Kevin Rich?"

Hal accelerated up the quiet street, speeding along the winding roads past beautiful homes on oversized lots. "We are." He handed me a small piece of notepaper, folded in half. I opened it and read the sentence scrawled across the page. *Kev's in Deer Hollow*.

"Where'd you get this?" I asked my PI.

"Will handed it off when he shook my hand. He didn't seem to want his dad to know he'd passed it."

"Curious," I mumbled.

"Yes, it is, isn't it? But even more curious...why is Kevin Rich in Deer Hollow? And is it just a coincidence he was there when another girl died?"

11

Hal's phone rang as we pulled into Deer Hollow. He glanced at the screen and frowned. "IMPD."

I felt my eyes go wide. "Why's the Indianapolis Metropolitan Police Department calling you?"

"Only one way to find out." He answered the call on speaker, putting his finger over his lips to indicate he wanted me to stay silent. "Hal Amity."

"Mr. Amity, this is Detective Brita Muldane. How are you tonight?"

"I'm fine, Detective. How can I help you?"

"I'm the detective in charge of the Brenda Wallace murder investigation. I'm sure you're familiar with it."

"I am."

"Yeah," the woman said, her tone dry. "I figured,

since I just got a call from the father of one of the persons of interest, accusing me of siccing the Deer Hollow police on his son."

Hal frowned. I made an "oops" face.

"As I told Mr. Zola, I'm not representing the police. I'm representing a client who has an interest in the case."

The woman on the other end laughed. "That's one way to put it. Your brother certainly does have an interest. In fact, he's lucky he's not cooling his heels in jail right now. I hear there's been another drug-related death."

Hal scrubbed a hand over his face. I knew what he was thinking. He'd inadvertently brought Asher exactly the kind of interest he'd been hoping to avoid. "Asher had nothing to do with either girl's death," he told Detective Muldane. "I'm just trying to get underneath what happened, so he doesn't get dragged into it."

A brief silence told me the detective was probably trying to decide if she was going to be offended by his implication that she didn't know how to find the guilty party. She finally sighed. "Look, I get the whole family and brother thing. My fiancée has seven brothers and, believe me, they don't like to follow the rules either when they're feeling protective. I get it. But you need to trust that I know what I'm doing and keep your nose out of my investigation. I can't have you riling up my suspects."

"Technically, I just riled up his father."

Muldane laughed. "Are you sure you're not a Honeybun?"

I scrunched my nose, mouthing "Honeybun?"

Hal shook his head. "A gooey breakfast pastry?"

"No, sorry, inside joke. Mr. Amity, this was a courtesy call. If you involve yourself in my investigation again, I'll be calling Deputy Willager next. Do we understand each other?"

"Perfectly." Hal let a beat of silence break between them and then asked, "What can you tell me about Kevin Rich?"

She laughed. "I can tell you he's none of your concern."

"Actually, he's just made himself my concern," Hal said as he pulled into the drive at my house.

"How's that?" she asked.

"He's standing in front of my girlfriend's home right now."

I was pretty sure that a few of the muffled words I barely understood were of the four-letter variety. Good ones too. Very creative. "Will you do me a favor and hand the phone to young Mr. Rich?"

Hal's smile was just a tad devilish. "Of course, Detective, just a min..." He punched the button to end the call, looking at me as he put the car into Park. "Oops."

I shook my head. "She's gonna be really cranky with you."

Hal shrugged. "Cranky females are nothing I haven't dealt with before."

I narrowed my eyes on him. "Surely you're not talking about me?"

He silenced his phone as it started to ring again. "Of course not." His grin widened. "I was referring to LaLee."

"Mm-hm." I couldn't help smiling as I watched him come around to open my car door for me.

As soon as my feet touched the ground, Hal turned and strode toward the young man standing next to a shiny black motorcycle, a helmet under one muscled arm. The kid had dark hair that fell into his eyes in a carefully orchestrated messy fringe. His eyes were a dark brown, like chocolate, and the thick arc of mahogany lashes gave his eyes a smoldering look.

His jaw was square, with stubble that matched his hair giving it good definition, and his nose, though slightly large for his face, was straight and attractive.

Kevin Rich looked like a kid from an upper-middle-class family who was used to getting pretty much everything he wanted. In his case, I wondered if looks were deceiving.

The kid stepped forward as Hal approached, offering him his hand. "Hey. You must be Hal." The teen smiled. "You look just like Ash."

Hal took the offered hand and gave it a brisk shake. "And I'm guessing you're Kevin Rich?"

"I am." He jerked his gaze toward me and gave me a crooked grin.

"I'm Joey," I told the kid, folding my arms over my chest instead of offering him my hand. Something about the kid was too smooth for my comfort. He was too self-assured. It probably had to do with the fact that he was so good-looking, and he clearly knew it. The girls probably threw themselves at his feet. It had made him cocky.

"What brings you to Deer Hollow, Mr. Rich?" Hal asked, his deep voice tinged with suspicion.

"I came to see Asher." He jerked his head toward the house. "Is he home?"

I frowned. "He's not staying here."

Rich looked surprised. "Oh. Sorry. This is the address he gave me."

I skimmed Hal a look, and he frowned. "Asher gave you this address?"

The kid nodded. "I tried calling him when I left Indy, but he didn't answer. He'd invited me to a party and told me he'd meet me here."

I couldn't read Hal's thoughts from his expression, but the kid's words certainly were a surprise to me. Asher hadn't mentioned inviting Kevin to the party, and he wouldn't have told him to come to my house if he had. "Are you sure he invited you?" I asked.

The kid laughed as if he thought I was stupid. "Of course." He frowned. "If you'll just tell me where he is, I'll get out of here."

Hal spoke before I could. "Why don't you come inside, Kevin. Maybe we can help straighten this out."

The kid didn't look happy with the prospect, but Hal clapped him on the back and headed for the house, pretty much towing him along.

High-pitched whining, followed by excited barking, preceded the sound of a muscular body slamming into the door as my pibl tried to defy the laws of physics and propel herself through a solid object to get to us.

The kid jerked to a stop and started backing away, his dark eyes wide. "That sounds like a really big dog."

"Oh, she's pretty big, but she's harmless," I said, laughing. "The worst she might do is knock you over trying to give you kisses."

The kid's eyes grew even wider. He started shaking his head. "No. I can't. I don't..." he reached up and touched a scar along his throat. It was about an inch long and barely noticeable under the porch light. I judged it to be an old scar. "I don't like dogs."

Hal looked at me. "Why don't you wait here, and I'll put her in your room?"

I nodded. "Come over here, Kevin, we'll sit for a minute while Hal puts Caphy away."

I sat in the swing and Kevin took a white wicker chair that faced out over the yard. It was the chair that was farthest from the front door. He kept giving the door worried glances as Hal fought his way past the energetic Pitbull and wrestled the door closed behind him.

The kid visibly relaxed as the door closed, his finger rubbing over the scar.

"Were you bitten once?" I asked him.

His gaze jerked to mine, filled with surprise. He apparently hadn't thought I'd pick up on the very obvious terror and the way his fear had made him focus on the scar. "Yeah. I was only five. I ran up to a dog at the park and tried to pet him without asking the owner if it was okay. The dog thought I was attacking him, I guess." He didn't look at me as he told the story. Either he was embarrassed or was afraid he'd see condemnation in my eyes for the mistake.

"Hal has a scar right here," I told him, indicating the track from the corner of my left eye to the ear on that side. Hal's scar was razor thin and barely visible. I mostly forgot he had it.

Kevin eyed the bruise on my temple, but he didn't ask me where I'd gotten it. "Was he attacked by a dog too?" he asked.

"I'm not sure. Every time I ask, he comes up with a new story. Between you and me, I think he was attacked by a cat. He really doesn't like them."

Though, I'd been joking, the kid thought I was serious. He shrugged. "I like cats."

We sat in silence for another minute, and then Hal opened the front door. "Coast is clear."

As I slipped past him, I could hear a very unhappy pibl scratching at my bedroom door, whining pitifully.

"She thinks she's dying," Hal said with a smile.

Kevin stood in the door listening to her nonsense. His expression was tight, his chest heaving.

I shared a look with Hal. "You know what? I can bring a snack out to the porch."

The kid's relief was obvious. "Okay, yeah. Thanks."

They went back outside, and I headed for the kitchen.

"Meow!" LaLee bounced down the stairs, her refuge having been invaded by a big, noisy canine, and followed me into the kitchen.

"Hey, pretty girl. Are you hungry?" I glanced at the clock. I'd fed them before we left, but I got the can of soft food out of the refrigerator and gave LaLee a dollop of the stinky stuff anyway.

I fixed a tray of small cupcakes and lemonade, adding napkins, and carried it out to the porch.

LaLee squeezed past me and bounded happily onto the porch before I could stop her.

Hal got up and took the tray from me.

"Thanks," I told him.

He settled it onto a small wicker table and handed Kevin a glass.

"Help yourself to some cupcakes," I told the kid, grabbing one myself before sitting down.

He took three of the bite-sized treats and settled back with a sigh. "It's nice here." He sounded surprised.

I gave him a teasing grin. "Let me guess, you thought there'd be pigs all over and stinkiness."

The kid stuffed a cupcake into his mouth, painting his upper lip with a dollop of white frosting. To his credit, he swallowed before answering. "Maybe a little."

I laughed. "Asher thought the same thing."

At the mention of his friend, Kevin frowned. "I really need to talk to him," Kevin said, addressing Hal. "Can you call him or something and tell him I'm here."

Hal stared at him a beat. "Ash didn't really invite you down, did he?"

The kid stuffed the last cupcake into his mouth. He licked frosting off his lips and shook his head. "I needed to see him. He didn't know I was coming." He put his lemonade back on the tray.

"Why?" Hal asked him. "Is something wrong?"

Kevin stared out over the yard, his big hands

clenched into fists on his thighs. "It's just that Ash left without telling us where he was going. I wanted to make sure he was okay."

"Why wouldn't he be okay?" Hal asked, his voice soft

The kid fidgeted, his hands clasping and unclasping on his thighs. He frowned. "Has there..." He shifted in his chair. "Has anybody showed up here? Anybody you didn't know?"

My guilty brain screamed Garland Medford's name and I chewed my lip, looking away.

"No," Hal responded. "Why do you ask?"

"No reason." The kid surged to his feet. "I gotta go."

Hal stood too. "Would you answer a few questions for me?"

The kid looked longingly toward his bike. "I really need to get..."

"Asher's in trouble, Kevin. He needs your help."

The kid's face was a study in fear. His body stiffened as his fingers clenched together hard enough to turn his knuckles white. He twisted his lips. "What happened?"

"Another girl overdosed, and the police think Asher sold her the drugs."

Kevin closed his eyes and dropped his head back. Then he opened them and slumped back into the chair, his shoulders rounding. "I knew it."

Hal and I shared a look.

"What did you know?" Hal asked.

The kid took a deep, shuddering breath and looked Hal in the eye. "I knew he wasn't done killing."

12

"He?" Hal sat forward in his chair. "Who's he?"

Kevin stared out into the night, his body rigid and his hands clasped tightly in his lap. He was the picture of stark fear. After a moment, he sniffed and I saw the silver trail of tears gliding down his ruddy cheek. "I don't know who he is. Nobody does, except the good-time girls."

I didn't like the sound of that. "Good-time girls?"

Kevin turned to me and nodded. "That's what we've been calling them. He seems to prefer girls. Maybe they're easier to convince, I don't know." Kevin shrugged.

"Convince of what?" Hal asked, his tone filled with unease.

"He recruits them to sell drugs for him. Lures them with money and expensive stuff."

"What kinds of expensive stuff?" I asked, thinking about Will Zola's shiny new motorcycle.

The kid shrugged. "Clothes, jewelry. One girl even got a car."

Hal and I shared a look.

"Was Brenda Wallace one of these good-time girls?" Hal asked Kevin.

"Yeah. She hit all the parties and even sold drugs at school."

"Did she use them too?"

"I'm not sure. One of my friends, a girl who Brenda approached to sell, said the girls weren't supposed to use the drugs themselves. Brenda told her they'd lose their slots if they did."

"Slots?"

Kevin looked at me. "That's what they call the jobs. These girls see it as a badge of honor to be picked for this. It's all a big game to them. And there's enough money and stuff to keep them hooked."

"Did your friend take one of the slots?" Hal asked.

"No. Her brother almost died from an overdose when she was a kid. She wants nothing to do with that lifestyle."

I wondered if Brita Muldane knew about this girl. She might be able to tell them something about the guy running the operation. "Did your friend tell the police?"

He shrugged. "Probably not. There's an undercurrent of 'we don't talk about this, or else' with that group. Besides, her family moved away a few months ago. I have a feeling she told her parents about Brenda's invitation, and they decided that getting their family away from the situation was the safest."

Hal nodded as if he agreed with that assessment. "How far-reaching is this operation?"

"I heard rumors of girls in Chicago and Cincinnati, maybe even Louisville. At least, that's what somebody told Brenda. It could all be bull."

"Why did you really come here tonight, Kevin?" Hal asked, his voice gentle.

The kid sighed. "When Ash disappeared...I was worried about him."

"You thought something bad had happened to Ash?" Hal's emerald gaze seemed darker under the porch lights. His jaw was tight with worry.

"He didn't tell me he was leaving." Kevin shrugged, trying to act like his coming to Deer Hollow hadn't been a big thing.

"He didn't exactly have a choice," Hal told the kid. He smiled sadly. "It was kind of an intervention."

"I figured." Kevin gave him an equally sad smile back.

"Do you think Will Zola is involved in selling drugs?" I asked.

"I don't know. I hope not."

Yet he'd pointed the police toward Will. "Why did you tell the police Will might be guilty?"

The kid bristled. "I didn't tell them that. They jumped to that conclusion all by themselves."

"Because of his brother, Penn?" Hal asked.

The teen twitched, his eyes skittering everywhere but at Hal or me. "Penn's a good guy."

"Maybe he is," Hal said. "But that doesn't answer my question."

Kevin stood up. "I gotta go. Tell Ash I stopped by and have him call me when he gets a chance." He strode quickly off the porch and grabbed the helmet off the seat of his bike, buckling it on.

Hal moved over to the steps and stood watching him. "If Penn Zola's involved and you're protecting him, you can be charged with aiding and abetting on these murders," Hal told the kid.

Kevin stilled, his gaze locked on the seat of his bike. "If Penn's involved, he's not the big guy."

"How do you know?" Hal asked him.

"Somebody would talk if it was Penn. They know him. They know his history."

"If you had to guess who the head of this organization was, who would you pick?"

Kevin's gaze rose to Hal's. "Probably somebody nobody knows. Maybe he's from Chicago or something." The teen shook his head, climbing onto the bike. "I want this guy caught as much as you do, Mr. Amity. He's killing my friends."

We watched the bike's headlamps cut through the darkness along the drive as he circled around. The arcs of light glanced off a deer and her fawn near the pond, sending them loping gracefully away.

A moment later, the kid turned his bike onto Goat's Hollow Road and accelerated, spitting gravel up behind him as he went.

Hal turned toward the house, his steps quick.

"What now?" I asked as I collected the tray.

"Now I do some research on the Zola family. And then I need to stop into the Sheriff's Office and talk to Ash."

I nodded and moved past him as he opened the door and ushered me inside. Weariness hit me with the suddenness of a lightning bolt. It had been a long day.

And it looked like it was going to be a long night too.

Asher sat slumped over the scarred wooden table in Interview Room A. He'd laid his head on his arms and his midnight hair, so like his brother's, was tousled as if he'd been continually running his fingers through it.

He didn't look up as Hal and I came through the door. Or when I set the bag with burgers and fries and a large soda in front of him.

Hal sat down next to Asher, and I took a chair across the table.

When he heard the screech of his brother's chair moving closer, the teen finally lifted his head. His dark green eyes were rimmed in red, the lids slightly puffy. The tip of his perfect Greek nose was red, and as he lifted his head he sniffed, running the back of his hand under it. Asher frowned at the bag. "Does this mean I have to stay here?"

Hal pushed it toward him. "Eat. You'll feel better."

"Doubt it," the kid mumbled, but he opened the bag and pulled out a burger. "Did you figure out who sold that girl the drugs yet?"

Hal leaned back, stretching his long legs out in front of him, and scrubbed a hand over his face. He looked tired. It had been a long day for him too. "I'm more concerned with why you had drugs in your pocket."

Asher swallowed, rubbing his lips with a paper napkin. "I swear they weren't mine."

"How did they get in your pocket?" Hal asked.

The kid frowned, the burger still clutched in two hands. "The party was cray. I was always bumping into people. Somebody must have slipped them into my pocket then."

"Did you bump into the victim?"

"I don't think so."

Hal nodded. "I need you to make a list of all the people you can remember bumping into."

Asher swallowed a bite. "I don't know any of their names."

"I'll see if Ame can come in and work with you."

Asher nodded, hope flaring in his gaze. He ate another big bite of burger and some fries. When his mouth was clear, he said, "The drugs weren't in my pocket when I got to the party, I know that."

"How can you be sure?" I asked.

Asher looked at me. "I ran my jeans through the wash last night. I always check my pockets before I throw them in the wash."

My lips twitched. "Really? I thought guys just threw whatever in the wash in a big wad and hoped for the best." I hadn't even conquered remembering to empty pockets myself. I was always finding shredded tissues from the pockets of my pants and shirts in the dryer.

Hal's smile was sad. "I believe him. Mom made us start washing our own clothes once we turned twelve. If she found a bunch of random stuff in the filter or the machine afterward, she would make us clean it up and she'd ground us. We learned pretty quickly to empty our pockets."

Asher swallowed another bite, his lips curving into a tired smile. "Remember when Cal left that bottle of ink from art class in his pocket?" The kid shuddered as Hal laughed.

"People thought Indy had an earthquake that day," Hal told me. "But it was just mom exploding over the ruined dryer."

"It took Cal three months of yard work around the neighborhood that summer to pay for a new dryer," Asher agreed. "He wore ink-splotched clothes to school for the rest of the year."

"His underwear looked like they were made of leopard skin." Hal and Asher shared a laugh that eased the lines of worry on their faces.

"The guys on the football team started calling him Tarzan," Hal told me, wiping tears of laughter from his eyes. "Good times."

I chuckled. "I guess having two older brothers probably saved your fanny a few times, huh?" I asked the kid. "Took the pressure off?"

Asher snorted. "No doubt."

With the release of some of the tension in the room, Hal sighed. "Are you sure you can't think of anyone who might have gotten close enough to you at the party to put those pills into your pocket?"

The kid chewed thoughtfully. "I mostly stayed with Ame. She introduced me to some of her girl-friends." He grimaced. "They're a really huggy group."

I hid a smile, having no doubt a bunch of high school girls would use any excuse to catch the attention of a kid as gorgeous as Asher Amity.

"They all kind of ran together after a while," he said.

Poor girls. Apparently, their ploy to entice Asher had failed. From what I'd seen of him and Ame together, he'd probably only had eyes for her. "Did Ame know the victim very well?" I asked.

"She was pretty upset when she saw who it was," Asher responded, grimacing. "It was an ugly scene."

"Who found her?" Hal asked.

The kid suddenly found a scratch on the table really interesting.

Hal sighed. "It was you?"

Asher looked miserable. "The party was in the back yard. Ame was cold, so I offered to get her sweater out of the car."

"And you saw the body in the bushes?"

Asher nodded. "I went over there, asking if she was okay. But she didn't answer me. That's when I got closer and..." He lifted a worried gaze to Hal. "I walked into the mulch and touched her. Do you think I left footprints and stuff?"

Judging by Arno's insistence on keeping Asher at the station, I was pretty sure he had.

"Tell me what you saw," Hal said.

Asher frowned. "Can't you ask that cranky cop? What a grump. I thought you two were friends."

To keep from smiling, I chewed the inside of my lip at Asher's description of Arno.

"We are. But he can't tell me anything about the body because I'm your brother."

"Then how are you gonna help me?" Asher asked, clearly panicking at the news.

"I've got ways," Hal told his brother. "I'm a private investigator. You hired me to investigate. As long as I don't interfere with Arno's case, he won't do anything about it."

The kid relaxed, nodding. "Okay."

"So tell me what you saw."

The kid pushed the food away, and his shoulders rounded. Shoving his hand through his hair, he swallowed. "She was laying in the mulch between two bushes. Her face was shoved into a prickly bush, and she had..." He swallowed again, looking a little green. He made a circle in front of his face with one finger. "Scratches all over her face."

"Go on," Hal urged, his tone gentle.

"The flowers around her feet were all mashed and torn up, her heels were dug into it like she'd been thrashing around."

We waited while he tunneled through his hair again. He pointed to his throat. "There were red marks on her throat."

Hal went very still. "Marks? You mean like she was strangled?"

Asher didn't seem to hear him. "Her eyes were open. Wide. They looked bulgy..." He gave a little sob and dashed angrily at the tears sliding down his face. "It was horrible."

Hal put a hand on his brother's shoulder. "What did you do then?"

"I had to see if she was alive," Asher squeaked out. He looked at Hal for apparent affirmation and his brother nodded.

"I knelt down next to her and felt..." He swallowed again. "I felt her throat, but I couldn't feel anything. She was..." He shuddered. "As soon as I realized she was dead, I backed out of there and called the cops."

"That's good, Ash," Hal told the kid, squeezing his shoulder. "Anything else?"

Asher put his head in his hands and stared at the table for a long moment. "Her shoe was off..." He blinked. "I saw something shiny underneath it."

"Like metal?" Hal asked.

The kid shook his head. "Not like that. It was more like..." His head lifted, and he snagged his brother's gaze with widened eyes. "Like plastic. Like a plastic bag."

Hal squeezed the kid's shoulder again. "Okay, Ash. I'm going to go now. But I'm working on this, you understand? I won't stop until I find out what really happened."

The kid took a deep breath and nodded. "Thanks."

Hal ushered me out the door ahead of him and looked back at his brother. "Do you need anything?"

"Yeah. Could you bring me a change of clothes from home? Maybe some snacks?"

"I can do that. I'll bring them by later." Hal stepped out into the hall and looked at me, his eyes hard.

"What is it?" I asked.

He took my arm and guided me away from the door. "I need to talk to Arno."

"Okay. But why? You're making me really nervous."

Hal led me down the hall toward Arno's office. "From what Asher told me, Rhonda Mae Gardner might not have died of an overdose as Arno implied. And if that's the case, Arno has no evidence at all that Asher killed her."

13

"Come in."

Hal turned the knob and placed a hand in the small of my back to usher me in ahead of him.

Arno was standing with his back to the door, hands on hips and gaze following the rush of traffic on the highway in the distance. It was a nearly constant stream of headlights and semi-trucks heading South toward Kentucky.

He turned as Hal closed the door behind us. His handsome face was set into an unreadable mask, his posture stiff as he indicated the chairs in front of his desk. "You talked to your brother?"

"I did. Now I need to talk to you."

Arno's jaw tightened at the accusation barely contained beneath Hal's statement. "Oh? You have a problem?"

"I do have a problem. Why didn't you tell me Rhonda Mae Gardner was strangled?"

Arno let his brows lift. "First of all, it's not your investigation. I believe I made it clear you couldn't be part of it. Secondly, we aren't sure yet, which killed her first. She definitely overdosed on the drugs."

"If she died of strangulation, you have no evidence against Asher for her murder."

"Technically, that's true," Arno agreed. To my surprise, he stood up and started pacing behind his desk. He clenched his hands into fists, worked his jaw, and then shoved his hands into the pockets of his uniform slacks as if he wasn't sure what to do with them. "Believe it or not, I'm not trying to convict your brother, Hal."

Hal sighed, scrubbing a hand over his jaw. "Has he seen his lawyer yet?"

Arno's derisive snort, followed by the curling of his top lip told me he had. "We really need to try to entice better lawyers to Deer Hollow," Arno said. He came around his desk and sat on the edge, crossing muscular arms over his chest. "Shulz is a total azzhat."

"I can't disagree," Hal said. He stared at his hands for a long moment. "What was the cause of death, Arno?"

"As I said, we don't know for sure yet..."

"Cut the CYA. What do you believe it was?"

Arno fixed Hal with a long look, his gaze hostile. When he answered, he ground the words out through stiff lips. "The general consensus, without the ME's final report, is death by asphyxiation."

Hal's shoulders relaxed. We sat in silence for a long moment. Then Hal looked up at the cop. "I spoke to Will Zola and his father tonight."

Arno nodded. "I'm aware. I got an angry call from Detective Muldane."

"I spoke to her too," Hal admitted. "I was very clear to Zola that I wasn't working with you."

"Zola's dealing with some stuff," Arno said, pursing his lips.

"You know him?"

"I know of him. Brita's report on the family was very thorough. Zola comes from a wealthy family. His father was very active in Indianapolis city politics before he died. Because of his alliances with people in power, all the way up to the Mayor, the family still has a lot of clout in Indianapolis. By all accounts, he was hard on his son. And William, a.k.a. Bill Zola didn't always measure up. It seems that he's coping with some personal things aside from having his kid mixed up in a drug-related murder."

"What kinds of things?" I asked, unable to stay quiet any longer.

Arno skimmed me a glance. "His wife left him a year ago, disappeared without a word. Then his older son, Penn, the product of a brief affair when

Zola was a newly married man, got into trouble with drugs and went to prison."

"From what Asher told us, Penn's turned out okay," I offered.

"It looks that way on paper, yes. He's even leading a drug addiction support group in a local church basement."

"But?" Hal urged.

"But, the speculation is that William Zola's having big financial trouble. His software company filed for Chapter 7 bankruptcy this year."

I sat forward. "How is that tied to Penn's issues?"

"Muldane believed Penn might have returned to his old ways to help his dad financially."

"Zola's close to Penn?" I asked.

"He is. Despite the questionable nature of his birth, Zola adopted him at age three when the kid's real mother skipped out on him. He's lived with the Zolas since then."

I arched a brow. "That must have been fun for the missing Mrs. Zola."

Arno didn't comment.

"So Muldane's working theory is that Penn's the one giving these girls drugs and killing them?"

"As I told you before, he does have an alibi. I'm not saying it's ironclad, but with Zola's exemplary behavior since getting out of prison, it gets harder to see him as the brains behind this drug thing." Arno shook his head. "None of this makes any sense. If he's selling drugs to these girls, why kill them? It's not good business, and it brings the wrong kind of attention to your operation."

Hal and I shared a look. "There's a story behind these girls and the drugs," Hal told Arno.

"Oh?"

"Kevin Rich turned up at Joey's house tonight."

Arno sat forward. "Go on."

Hal told Arno what the teen had told us. When he was done, the cop was frowning thoughtfully. "Do we know when Rich arrived in Deer Hollow?"

"Do you mean, could he have been the one to kill Rhonda May?"

Arno nodded.

"I don't know the answer to that. It's certainly something to consider. It's only about a forty-five minute drive back to the Rich's home. He wouldn't necessarily have to be staying here."

"What do you think about the kid's story?" Arno asked us.

"It's plausible," I said. "Even with a culture of enforced silence between the good-time girls, somebody would be more likely to talk if the recruiter was Penn. They know him. They know his history. They might be less likely to trust their lives to him because of his past and the fact that he's gone to prison for what he did."

"Kevin thought it was probably someone the

girls didn't necessarily know before he recruited them," Hal added.

"Well, that rules all of our potential suspects out." Arno stood up and returned to his spot in front of the window. "We don't seem to be making any progress."

Hal reached over and clasped my hand.

Guilt ate at me. I could definitely see Garland Medford in the role of a charismatic older man who could buy a bunch of starry-eyed teenaged girls glittery gifts to entice them to do his bidding. That, and his reputation as a mobster, no matter how distinguished he appeared, made him the perfect suspect.

And I hadn't told Hal he'd been in town. Or that he'd come to see me.

We sat in taut silence for a long moment while guilt twisted my belly into painful knots.

When the silence became too much, I opened my mouth to blurt out a confession.

Arno turned abruptly from the window. "I'll release Asher on his own recognizance. You can take him home. But I expect you to bring him back if or when it becomes clear he has something to answer to in this investigation."

Hal stood up, relief clear in his expression. "Thanks, Arno."

I stood too, though I wasn't feeling nearly as relieved as Hal. He touched my arm, gently urging me toward the door. But I dug in my heels. "I can't leave yet."

Hal frowned. "What's wrong, Joey?"

I turned to Arno. "There's something I need to tell you." My gaze slid to Hal. "Both of you. And you're not going to like it."

"What is it?" Arno asked, frowning.

I could feel Hal's gaze on me as I took a deep breath and told them about Garland Medford's visit after my attack. When I was done, both men were silent for a beat. I finally risked a glance at Hal.

His impossibly handsome face was tight, anger seething in his green eyes. I winced. "I'm sorry I didn't tell you. But Medford convinced me it would be dangerous if I told anyone."

"Dangerous how?" Arno asked.

Hal continued to be silent and it worried me.

"He said there were people who wouldn't like him sticking his nose in." Filled with a burning need to know where we stood, I turned to Hal. "Say something."

He stared at the floor, his lips pressed into a tight line. "I'm assuming this is where your odd question earlier came from?" He looked at me, anger darkening his gaze.

"What question?" Arno asked.

Hal's gaze stayed on me as he responded. "She asked if it was possible the person who is behind the drugs in Indy could have come to Deer Hollow to get at Asher."

"Garland said Asher was in danger," I said, my tone more pleading than I liked. "And after I was attacked in the woods..."

Hal blinked, realization filling his expression. He closed his eyes. "Medford could have been here when you were attacked."

I sighed, dropping into the nearest chair. "Yeah. Believe me, I've thought of that."

Arno picked up the phone and started punching numbers.

"Who are you calling?" Hal asked, finally looking away from me.

Arno held up a finger as he spoke into the phone. "Brita? We have a new development here. I need to know if you've looked at Garland Medford in your investigation." Arno listened for a moment, and his eyes went wide. He shot us a look. "When?" He listened for another minute and then turned away, staring out his window. Finally, he sighed. "Any leads?"

I glanced at Hal, and he shook his head. He didn't have any idea what the detective could be telling Arno.

"Okay, let me know if anything changes." Arno disconnected the call and turned around, his cell clutched forgotten inside a white-knuckled grip. The skin around his lips was white. Weariness painted every line of his big form.

"What's happened?" Hal asked.

"Garland Medford is probably a dead end." He laughed bitterly. "Poor choice of words."

Dread prickled in my chest, tightening my lungs until I had to work to pull air into them. "What happened?"

Arno held my gaze, his expression grim. "Garland Medford was killed about an hour ago."

14

I stared at Arno in shock, unable to form words or thoughts to respond. *Garland dead? Was it real?* He'd been the boogie man in my life for so long, it didn't seem possible he could be gone. Could the threat he'd represented to my family really be ended?

I realized I should feel relief. But I didn't. A man was dead — a man who'd stood in front of me mere hours earlier and offered me information that would protect Hal's brother.

Was it possible Medford hadn't been the monster I'd always believed him to be? It was the kind of thought I'd had several times over the last few months. I'd always blamed him for my parents' deaths. Then, when I'd discovered my mom wasn't dead, I'd worried he'd come after her to finish the job I'd thought he'd started. But he hadn't. And he'd told me he knew she was alive. He'd told me several times that he wasn't my enemy...*her* enemy. But I hadn't believed him.

And he was dead.

I gasped as I had a sudden, terrible thought. Could he have been killed because he'd come to warn me? What if I'd inadvertently caused his death?

My head jerked up, and I fixed Arno with a look that felt slightly desperate. "How'd he die?"

"He ran his car into a telephone pole. The car burst into flames and he didn't make it out. Muldane believes he was run off the road. The left rear quarter panel of his car was crushed."

He'd been murdered...

"Do the police know who killed him?" Hal asked.

Arno shook his head, his expression thoughtful. "From what Joey said, I'm guessing it's possible the person behind these murders caught up to him. If that's what happened, Medford was right. The person behind the drugs and deaths is one ruthless SOB."

I felt Hal's gaze on me and turned. He looked worried. "Asher and Joey are in trouble," he told Arno.

I shook my head. "I'm not in trouble. Why would you think that?"

"Because you were attacked on your own property," Hal said. "Until we know why, we have to assume you've somehow found your way into this guy's crosshairs."

Arno sat down at his desk, pulling his computer closer. "Get your brother home, Amity. I suggest you stay at Joey's. That cabin of yours is too isolated. Until we get to the bottom of the attack and Medford's death, we need to assume you're all targets."

"That's just perfect," I muttered as Hal took my elbow and gently pried me from the chair. I forced a smile a few minutes later as we all headed toward Hal's car. "We're going to have a sleepover. Fun."

Asher rolled his eyes. "Can I call Ame and have her come over too?"

Hal peaked a brow as he opened the car door and gave me a hand into the big car. "Not for a sleepover."

Asher huffed. "I just meant to hang out for a while."

"I don't know. We'll see."

Asher slumped unhappily in the back seat. Typical teenager. He'd been sprung from jail, and all he could do was get irritated about not having his way about the next thing.

At that moment, I was soooo happy to be an only child.

"Can we at least stop by the cabin and get my stuff?" he whined.

"We can certainly do that," Hal said. He turned to me with a grin. "If we hurry we can just about make it to Sonny's before they close. How about we pick up carryout slices of pie?"

I eagerly agreed. "I'm in. But we should probably get a whole pie. We might be hunkering down for a while." I would immerse myself in sweet, creamy goodness and try to shove the ugly out of the world for a while.

Okay, maybe teens weren't the only ones who were always looking to the next thing they wanted.

But...pie.

B y the time we got home, it was eleven pm. We decided it was too late for Asher to call Ame about coming over. So we ate our pie in front of one of my favorite CSI shows, Hal and I snuggled on the couch with LaLee draped over the back, and Asher, Caphy, and Ethel Squeaks all piled together on the floor amid a mound of blankets and pillows.

True to her nature, Ethel tried to hog the blankets — pardon the pun — and carry the pillows off to her tent. Hal and I laughed at the battle between her and Asher, especially when Caphy decided the pillow they were fighting over looked like a fun toy and dove into the middle of the fight, her tail glee-fully whacking Asher upside the head.

Despite his feigned indignation, I could tell the kid was happy to be back amid the craziness, and the sight of him playing with the animals warmed the cockles of my heart every bit as well as the pie warmed the gastric cockles of my rounded belly.

Finally, after much jockeying for position, the three of them settled down together. One of Asher's arms was draped over Ethel's new red ball because she refused to let him move it.

I enjoyed the silence for a few minutes, and then Caphy and Ethel started to snore.

Asher looked up at me with despair in his familiar green gaze.

I laughed until tears wet my cheeks.

The kid just shook his head at me.

Hal pulled me close, kissing me on the forehead as he settled in with a sigh.

I woke up to the sun heating the room around me. Caphy's snoring still rumbled on the morning air. Birds sang beyond the open window of my bedroom and I stretched, yawning widely.

I didn't remember coming to bed. Hal must have carried me up and tucked me in. I looked down to find myself still dressed in my stretchy shorts and tee. I hadn't even showered.

My teeth felt kind of gritty, and I grimaced as I

thought of the sugar from the pie sitting on them all night.

Pie! Maybe there was some left in the fridge.

With happy thoughts of having dessert for breakfast, I trudged into the bathroom to shower and brush my teeth. When I bounced down the steps twenty minutes later, Caphy nearly took my feet out from under me on her headlong dash to the door.

I let her out as my nose perked to the scent of frying bacon.

Like a zombie, I headed toward the delectable scent, shuffling along and making growly noises the cast of The Walking Dead would have envied.

To my complete shock, Asher was standing at the stove, my favorite spatula clutched in his hand and his dark hair sticking up in messy spikes.

Yes, I do have a favorite spatula. Don't you?

Asher turned as I groaned in delight. "Hey. You okay?"

I rubbed my temples. "Headache," I said, not wanting to admit I'd been moaning for bacon. A girl has to guard her pride. "Where's your brother?"

The kid scooped the bacon from the pan and layered it over a stack of paper towels on a plate. "He's in the living room. Working."

I made like a zombie toward the coffee, popping a pod of my favorite brew into the machine and hitting the button. "Did you sleep okay?"

Asher stirred a pan filled to the brim with scrambled eggs. "The pig kept stealing the blankets."

I grinned. "Maybe you should sleep in her tent tonight and let her have the nest in front of the TV."

"Ha!" he said, a smile twitching on his lips.

"What can I do to help?"

"Make toast?"

"You got it."

Footsteps sounded behind me. "Morning." Hal kissed me on the lips and then headed to the fridge. "I'll pour juice." He pulled out a bottle of orange juice and set it on the counter, retrieving three small glasses and filling them. "How'd you sleep?" he asked me.

The toast popped up, and I sliced off a sliver of butter, spreading it over a hot slice. "Like the dead. How about you?" Hal had insisted on sleeping on the couch rather than in one of my guest rooms. Probably because they were kind of a mess. I'd turned one into an exercise space and the other had become a dumping ground for all the stuff I needed to take to the attic but was too lazy to carry up.

"I caught a few winks in between the snoring. Your head's not bothering you?" Hal asked.

"When I think about it, yeah. But the pain meds are doing a pretty good job."

"Good."

"That bruise has reached a pretty interesting color," Ash said.

It was the first time he'd mentioned anything having to do with my attack. I had put it down to being understandably tied up in worries about his own fate, given what had happened at the party and afterward.

"My goal is to achieve hues across the gamut of colors," I joked. I studied Hal as he settled juice near each plate, attempting to figure out if he was mad at me for not telling him about Medford.

Medford!

My knees wobbled and I had to lean against the counter as it hit me that my arch-nemesis was dead. Horror made my stomach twist until a second, happier thought followed.

My mother could come home! To my surprise, the thought made fresh worry whirl in my belly.

"What's the plan for today?" Asher asked.

I finished buttering five slices of toast and headed to the table with them. Asher had placed overflowing plates of eggs and bacon next to the napkins and silverware Hal had arranged. I sat down with my coffee, sighing with pleasure. "This looks delicious." I cast Hal's brother a look. "Where did you learn to cook?"

He tucked a bite of eggs into his mouth, giving me a wry smile. "Mom gave up on having a girl when I was born. She was forced to treat me like the daughter she'd never have. It's been the bane of my existence being the last. On the flip side, I do a mean cross-stitch."

Hal chuckled. He sat back in his chair, sipping his coffee but not eating. "I really wish cell phones had been a thing when he was growing up. That pink, sparkly tutu costume at Halloween was priceless. Though he kept tripping over the toe shoes."

My eyes went wide. "No. She didn't."

Asher sighed. "Mom didn't dress me in the tutu, no." He glared at his brother. "This ape and the other monkey did. I was only three, so I'm not permanently scarred by the experience. But close."

I hid a smile behind my juice glass.

Hal picked up a slice of bacon and nibbled it. He looked thoughtful.

"What are you thinking so hard about?" I asked him.

"Ame."

Asher's brows lifted. "Huh?"

"We need to talk to her about the victim."

His brother frowned. "Why?"

"Because Ame might know who Rhonda Mae was working with. She might have information she doesn't even realize she has. Maybe Rhonda Mae said something. Or one of the kids saw her talking to someone." He shrugged. "As you know, teenaged girls like to talk about each other."

"Ame's not like that," Asher said, sipping his own coffee.

"Then maybe she can tell us who we need to talk to. She was at the party, Ash. She knew the victim. We need to talk to her."

Asher didn't look happy about it. "I don't want you dragging her into this."

"What you want isn't important," Hal said, his tone dismissive. "A girl's dead."

Tension throbbed around the table until it killed my appetite. Setting down my fork, I said, "How about we invite her over here? We can talk to her, and then you guys can hang out for the day."

Asher seemed to be considering it. He lifted his gaze to Hal. "Can we take the 4-wheeler into the woods?"

"I don't see why not. As long as you stay on Joey's and my property."

"And get back before dark," I reminded, rubbing my head without thinking. "There are a lot of coyotes around here."

Asher nodded. "I'd like to show her that big building in the back if you don't mind."

"Not at all." I didn't think a teenaged girl would have any interest in an old metal building, but I didn't want to dampen his enthusiasm. Ame would probably enjoy the space just because he so clearly did.

"Good," Hal said, standing with his empty plate. "I'm going back to work. You'll call her?" he asked his brother.

Asher nodded. He chewed thoughtfully, watching Hal as he left the kitchen. I realized with a start that I was watching him too.

My face must have revealed my worry.

"Is something wrong?" Asher asked.

I jerked my gaze his way, held the inquisitive dark green eyes for a beat, and then looked away. "It's nothing."

"He's not mad."

I raised my eyes. "What?"

"Hal. He's not mad. If he was, he'd say something to your face. He doesn't hold that kind of thing in."

The kid was right. I knew he was. I sighed. "Maybe it's just my guilt talking."

Asher nodded. "Medford can be a pretty persuasive guy."

Ash had no doubt listened to us talking about Medford on the ride home the night before. Hal hadn't gotten testy with me about my silence regarding Medford's visit. But he'd let me know he wasn't happy about the omission.

I blinked in surprise. "You knew Medford?"

Asher nodded. "Yeah. We all do...did."

"How?"

Asher set his fork next to his plate and picked up his coffee. "Medford has a bad rep, but he's not...he wasn't a bad guy. He sponsored an after-school program for troubled teens. He even built an indoor recreational park with basketball and soccer facilities and a climbing wall for us. He didn't do it to get credit. He didn't put his name on any of it. He did most of it anonymously."

"But you knew?"

"Yeah. Like Hal said, kids like to gossip."

I thought about that for a while. What if I'd been wrong about Medford all this time? Then Asher's words struck me. "You said he built it for troubled teens?"

Asher nodded.

"Did they provide counseling services there?"

"I think so. Nobody I knew ever went."

"Do you know who the counselor was?"

"Nah." Asher got up and took his plate to the sink, rinsing it and dropping it into the dishwasher like Hal had.

The Amity boys had been raised right. If I ever met Hal's mom, I needed to tell her that. The thought exploded like dynamite in my belly. A terrifying idea...meeting his mom.

Scratch that all to heck and back.

"What's the name of the center?" I asked, nudging him away from the sink.

"Brighter Day Youth Center," he told me, wrinkling his nose. "Stupid name."

"I'll wash the pans," I told him. "You can go call Ame if you want."

I waited for Asher to leave the kitchen and then

grabbed my cell phone. I dialed, and it rang several times before a man's voice answered. "Hello?"

"Reverend Smythe?"

"This is he."

"It's Joey Fulle. How are you, pastor?"

"Joey, what a nice surprise. We've missed you at services."

I winced. I hadn't gone to church much since I lost my parents. You could say I'd had a crisis of spirit from their loss. Reverend Smythe had been kind and patient with me, always letting me know I was welcome at Deer Hollow Lutheran Church. But lately, he'd been getting more direct with his nudging. Every time I ran into him, he gave me some form of the same message. He was probably starting to lose hope that I'd ever return.

"Your Mr. Amity should bring you with him the next time he comes."

I nearly swallowed my tongue. "My...?"

"But that's not why you called me, is it? How can I help?"

I swallowed a few times, trying to catch up to the rapid-fire conversational transformation. "Yes. Um, I wanted to talk about those meetings you have in the basement."

Silence met my statement. I could almost hear him wondering why I was broaching that subject.

"Do you need help, Joey?"

"I do, actually."

"Oh…"

"For an investigation. I thought, since you provide support meetings for alcoholics, you might know others in the area who offer the same thing? Maybe someone in Indianapolis? I know it's a long shot, but…"

"Not as long as you might think," he told me in a relieved voice. "Addiction counselors get together regularly for training and advice. Since there aren't many of us down here in the boonies," He chuckled. "I often go into Indianapolis for discussion and fellowship. Who were you wondering about?"

"I don't know his name. That's why I'm calling. But it would be someone who works at Garland Medford's recreational facility for troubled teens. Brighter Day Youth Center." I chewed nervously on my lip. The rev likely wouldn't know a secular counselor. He probably hung out with other religious leaders because they'd have more in common than a counselor at a secular facility.

"Ah, yes. That's Milo Dill's location. He's a fine man. Younger than me by a few decades, but he went to Seminary with my nephew. I actually spoke to him recently about a sponsorship opportunity. He's working with businesses in Indianapolis to offer a step up for deserving youth. He called to tell me he'd been authorized to give out one sponsorship in Deer Hollow. I was touched by his kind offer. Would you like his number?"

I definitely *would* like his number. I grinned. "Please." I jotted it down, thanked Reverend Smythe, and disconnected, feeling pretty good about myself.

Then I headed toward the living room to tell Hal what I'd found.

15

We discussed my information and decided, in the interests of not sticking our noses where they might get Arno's hands slapped again, to pass it on to him to pursue. Hal called Deputy Willager and gave him Milo Dill's name and number and our thoughts about why the counselor might be a useful person to talk to. When Hall hung up, he passed on Arno's "less than sincere" thanks with a grimace.

"Ame's on her way over," Asher told us.

Hal glanced up from his laptop and nodded. "Good. Thanks."

I sat on the couch next to him, a small, lined pad in my lap and a pen between my teeth. With two extra mouths to feed in the house, I was badly in need of a grocery run. I looked at Asher. "Any requests from the store?"

Asher's eyes lit. "More pie?"

I narrowed my gaze on him. "I'm guessing it was *you* who ate the last slice of pie last night."

The kid shrugged, not looking even a little bit ashamed for his larceny. "In my defense, I couldn't sleep because Ethel kept hitting me in the head with that stupid ball."

I twisted my lips to hide a smile. "She doesn't recognize the difference between two in the morning and two in the afternoon."

"Tell me about it." He gave me a disgusted look, but humor sparked in his gaze. "I finally had to bribe her into the kitchen with a piece of crust and close the door."

"Don't give the pig sweets," Hal said without looking up. "She's on a strict diet."

Ash threw Hal a look filled with disgust. "No wonder she's so annoying. She's probably manic with hunger."

I snorted out a laugh. "Hardly. She eats more than you and I combined..." Then I thought about the volume of food Asher consumed and grimaced. "Well. At least more than I do. She just eats her piggy pellets and fruit and vegetables. We're trying to keep her from becoming a tubby little piggy." I grinned as Ethel bounded into the room with Caphy hot on her hooves. She flipped the little red ball ahead of her, and Caphy bounced after it.

Ethel left the pibl hanging with the ball in her

mouth and her butt in the air, and ran over to Asher. She pressed herself against his calf, tail twirling coquettishly.

I grinned. "She likes you."

Asher tried to look disinterested, but he reached down and scratched the spikey tuft of hair between her big ears when he thought I wasn't looking.

"That reminds me," I said around the much-abused pen. "I need more fruit." I added apples, strawberries, melon, and bananas to my list. "When are you going to talk to Ame?" I asked Hal.

He sat back and gave me a warm look. "After lunch. I don't want to pounce on her as soon as she walks through the door."

Asher frowned. He really seemed worried about us talking to Ame. Apparently, Asher had the same protective streak as his older brother. I realized with a start that Asher was falling for Lis's pretty cousin. I wasn't surprised. Ame carried herself with an elegance and maturity that was rare for someone her age. Add her stunning beauty to the mix, and it was no wonder Asher was smitten.

I patted Hal's knee. "I'm going to run to Junior's. We're out of everything."

He nodded toward the notepad in my hand. "Did you add steaks to that list?"

"No. But that sounds good." I jotted the addition to the page and tore it off the pad. Folding it up, I shoved it into the pocket of my shorts. "I'll be back in about an hour."

"Pie!" Asher yelled as I shoved Caphy away from the door, kissed her on her wide nose, and slipped through a space that was wide enough for me but not the pibl trying to attach herself to my leg.

"Goodpie to you too!" I said, grinning. "See you in a bit."

J unior's Market was packed by Deer Hollow standards. Which meant there were five other cars in the lot when I parked my 2012 Jeep Wrangler Sport and climbed out. The day was perfect for mid-summer in Southern Indiana. The temperature was in the low eighties, and a cloudless blue sky hung over Deer Hollow. The town had tugged on a frilly skirt of happy colors via copious amounts of vibrantly hued flowers and bright green grass. As usual, the smell of freshly cut grass made me inhale deeply, the sweet scent like a trip back into memories of my mom mowing the grass around our house. I smiled at the reminiscence. All my friends' moms stuck to the inside chores, and their dads did the outside stuff. My mom never believed in a traditional division of labor. She liked putting on a sleeveless top and enjoying the heat of a bright summer day, carving perfect rows across the grass.

The rumble of mowers accompanied the sweet scent of grass as I pulled the door open, thinking I should get my mower out soon too. The heavier than usual rain we'd been experiencing recently was keeping everybody busy trying to tame our lushly-growing lawns.

I grabbed a cart and pushed it through the glass doors as they opened.

"Hello, Joey," a big man behind the customer service counter called out. I turned to find Junior Milliard, the owner of the small country store, waving at me.

"Hey, Junior."

He stepped out from behind the counter and strode quickly in my direction. Junior was in his mid to late-forties, with thinning brown hair, a ruddy complexion, and a soft middle. He was tall, well over six feet, and he looked even bigger because of the thirty or so extra pounds he carried around with him. Junior offered me his hand, grinning widely. "I haven't seen you in a while."

I shook the big, soft hand and returned his smile. "I'm a morning person. I generally come early in the day. You're usually not here yet."

He nodded, shoving his hands into the pockets of his mud-brown slacks. "I don't know if I ever thanked you for helping me save my store."

I shook my head. "I didn't really do anything." All I'd done was help Hal and Arno solve a mystery that involved a larcenous realtor, currently deceased, who'd thought it would be a good idea to engage in title theft of the businesses in Deer Hollow. When the realtor was killed as the result of her illegal antics, a judge returned the titles for the stolen businesses to their rightful owners.

"I appreciated you and Hal speaking up for me."

We'd also given a statement to the judge, which seemed to have helped sway his opinion. "We were happy to help."

Junior nodded. I was itching to get my shopping done and get back home, but he stood with his hands in his pockets and stared at my cart as if he had something else he wanted to say.

"Is there something wrong?" I asked him.

He shook his head. "I wanted to ask you about the girl."

"The girl?" Then it hit me. "You mean Rhonda Mae?"

His brown eyes found mine. "Do you know if they found who killed her yet?"

I glanced away, knowing I couldn't tell him what I knew even if I knew anything. "I don't know any more than you do, Junior. Arno's still investigating. I don't even know if she was killed. It could have been an accident."

He stared at me as if he didn't believe me. "I

know you and that PI are involved, Joey. I'm just asking for something to cling to. Some small hope for Rhonda Mae's parents."

The Deer Hollow gossip mill strikes again. "You knew her?"

Junior sucked air and expelled it slowly. "Rhonda Mae's dad has been my friend since grade school. He's really torn up about her death." Tears glistened in Junior's eyes. "She was their only child."

I reached out and squeezed Junior's thick arm. "I'm so sorry."

Junior sniffed. "John and I used to take her to the playground when she was little. His wife was a stay-at-home mom, and when he was home, he liked to give her a little break." Junior smiled sadly. "But he loved every minute of that time with Rhonda Mae."

I didn't know what to say to comfort him. "Were you aware she was using drugs?"

Junior jerked as if I'd struck him. "Not a chance. That girl didn't even take aspirin when she had a headache." He shook his head. "If she had drugs in her system, somebody else put them there."

Adults often didn't believe the teenagers they knew could do bad stuff. Parents usually had no clue that their very normal seventeen-year-olds would make out under the bleachers or drink at parties. They preferred to believe their kids were angels. "Could she have been hanging out with some bad kids?"

Junior shrugged. "If so, John didn't say anything about it. I think he'd have told me if he was worried about her."

He probably would have. "Arno will get to the bottom of this, Junior."

Junior nodded. "Thanks, Joey." He walked away, every line of his big body drooping with disappointment.

I had to force myself to turn away and start my shopping, or I'd be tempted to give him a sliver of hope that I had no right to offer.

A man came around the end of an aisle, moving fast, and his cart crashed into the side of mine. The sound of the two carts colliding was loud enough to draw the attention of everyone within sight in the store.

"Oh!" I jolted backward, instinctively trying to get out of his way.

The man looked to be in his early thirties or late twenties. His light brown hair was shorn close to his scalp, and he was dressed in loose jeans and a sloppy tee shirt. He looked down at the cell phone he'd dropped when we'd collided. From the partial text I could see on the screen, I suspected that was the reason he'd run into me.

Dark brows lowered as he examined the screen of the cell.

"You shouldn't text and drive," I told him in a teasing tone.

His head jerked up, and he fixed me with angry blue eyes. "Yeah, sure." And that was all he said. Without apology or even recognition of my joke, he maneuvered his cart around mine and moved on to the next aisle.

I stared after him. Then I glanced toward Junior, who was shaking his head at the man's rudeness.

I sighed and headed down a different aisle. I didn't know the man, which meant he was probably new in Deer Hollow. Hopefully, he was just having a bad day.

I added items on my list to my cart and forced myself past the cakes and pies. If I was going to spend calories on dessert, I wanted it to be worth eating. I'd pick up a whole pie from Sonny's on the way home.

I don't need you giving me a hard time!

I jerked to a stop at the angry tone of voice.

Of course I know what I'm doing. This has to be done.

The voice had come from the next aisle over and, though the man appeared to be trying to keep his voice low, anger made it carry. *He won't get a chance to tell that story. I promise you.*

The first bloom of alarm swirled through me.

Was he threatening somebody in Deer Hollow?

I had a sudden desire to see who was speaking and hurried forward. I was rounding the end of the aisle when the man who'd run into me before nearly hit me again.

"Jeez, lady, you're everywhere."

I blinked, struck to silence by the man's tone.

He still sounded angry. And he sounded just like the guy who'd been talking on the phone.

At my too-interested stare, the guy's gaze locked on mine and his eyes narrowed.

I quickly put my head down and moved past him down the aisle, feeling the sting of his assessing gaze between my shoulder blades as I hurried away.

What should I do? I had no proof the stranger had been threatening anyone, but I also didn't know what else he could have meant by the words; *He won't get a chance to tell that story.*

It was clearly a threat.

I heard the checkout clerk speaking to someone and peeked around the endcap. The man was checking out!

I waited while he paid, catching Junior staring at me as I hid behind the sale items on display. I shook my head as he opened his mouth to speak, and he turned a speculative gaze on the man who was walking out of the store.

With a look of apology, I left my cart and hurried after him. I forced myself to slow to a walk as I slipped through the automatic doors.

The man was just slamming the back door of an oversized black pickup truck when I hit the asphalt.

He saw me striding toward him as he opened the driver's side door. His gaze narrowed. He stiffened as if expecting trouble.

I gave him a smile. "Hello."

His brows lowered.

"I just wanted to welcome you to Deer Hollow." I stretched my smile as wide as I could, and it felt like a death mask.

The man's frown deepened. "How do you know I need welcoming?"

I let the smile fall away. "Oh. Sorry, did I offend you? It's just that, with all the new homes going up around here, I've been trying to reach out to new people to make them feel..."

"Welcome?" he ventured.

My laugh sounded forced.

He crossed his arms over his chest, peering down at me with amusement. "You're the welcome wagon lady?"

"Ha, ha. Sort of, I guess."

He spread his hands, glancing around. "No basket full of goodies? I feel slighted."

"Ha. Did you move into The Hollows? Those are nice homes."

He studied me. I forced myself not to fidget beneath his unfriendly gaze. Finally, he nodded.

I stuck my hand out. "I'm Joey Fulle."

Something passed through his gaze. Hostility? Distrust?

"I live on the other end of town."

After a long, uncomfortable beat, during which I could swear I felt ants crawling across my skin, he reached out and clasped my hand. "Name's Pendleton."

"It's nice to meet you, Mr. Pendleton. I hope you're enjoying Deer Hollow." I turned back toward the store. "Have a nice day."

"Miss Joey Fulle?"

I jerked to a stop, something cold slithering down my spine. I tried to plaster a smile on my face as I turned back. I didn't quite manage it. "Yes?"

"You don't happen to know a Hal Amity, do you?"

Oh, oh.

"I do. He's my..." Boyfriend sounded kind of weak. "Private Investigator."

The man lifted a brow. In the blink of an eye, he'd closed the distance between us. He bent down, his face too near mine, and wrapped fingers that were like bands of iron around my forearm. His lips curled. "You need your own private investigator?"

Um, yeah. I kind of did. On many levels. "He's a friend. A really good friend." I put emphasis on that last, a warning to the man trying to intimidate me.

I jerked my arm out of his grip, letting my hands drop to my sides so I wouldn't be tempted to rub the spot where he'd clutched me.

Pendleton stepped closer and, dang my nerves, I

took a step back. "You and Amity keep your noses out of my business, or you're going to be sorry."

"Joey?"

Pendleton's head jerked up and he spotted Junior. He gave the man a wave and, after a final glare in my direction, climbed into his truck and drove out of the lot.

I watched him turn north, realizing he wasn't heading to The Hollows at all.

Footsteps hurried up behind me. "Are you okay?" Junior asked. "Did he hurt you?"

Junior's wide face was red with anger.

"I'm fine."

His gaze slid down to the bruised flesh of my forearm, which I'd been rubbing without realizing. I hid the arm behind me. "Have you seen that guy around before?"

Junior nodded. "He's been in here a couple of times."

"How long has he been coming in?" I asked.

"A couple of days. I think he's staying out at the campground."

"Why do you think that?"

"He has a sticker on his truck window."

The campground. Of course. Hal and I had checked the hotels, but we hadn't thought to check the Deer Hollow Campground. I tugged my cell from my pocket.

"Do you want me to finish your shopping and deliver it to your house?" Junior asked.

"That would be great," I said, handing him the list. "Thanks, Junior."

He inclined his head. "I'll get it there within the hour. Will you be home?"

"Somebody will be there. Thanks again." I hurried to my Jeep.

Hal answered on the third ring. "Let me guess, they're out of banana cream pie?"

"I don't know. I never made it there."

Hal caught the intensity threading my voice. "What's wrong?"

"I think I just bumped up against my attacker."

There was a rustling on the other end that told me Hal was on the move. "Where is he?"

"He was in Junior's, but he's gone. I think I know where he went, though."

"I'll be there in ten minutes."

"No, wait there for me. I'm coming to you."

16

The Deer Hollow Campground was full to burstin'. Dozens of campers of all shapes and sizes lined up along its narrow asphalt drive, their noses pointed toward the large, green-blue expanse of the manmade swimming lake. The single drive wound around the lake, its backside picturesque with mature trees that provided beauty and shade for campers who weren't lucky enough to have snagged a waterside view of the unnaturally-hued swimming hole. Small, yappy dogs were tied to campers on the shade side, and older campers, most with sharp, inquisitive eyes and white to charcoal gray hair, watched us pass on by.

Kids dotted the small beach under the watchful eyes of their swimsuit-clad parents, their older siblings forming a small island of attitude and too-small swimwear as far down the sand as they could go without falling off the beach.

The teens gave off a veritable miasma of "I don't know those people"; from the distance they kept, to the way they avoided even looking toward the parental environs down the way.

I eyed the teenagers, wondering if any of them were locals. Probably not. I could only assume that if your preferred vacation was a trip to a campground, you'd at least pick one that was some distance away from your own backyard.

Hal drove the SUV slowly along the road, his eyes skimming the lakeside while mine scoured the shade side.

I didn't see a truck like the one Pendleton had climbed into, but then several of the campers were currently sans vehicles.

"Anything?" Hal asked as we reached the campground office.

"No."

He parked the Escalade. "I'll go inside and see if they'll give me a list of vehicles."

"'Kay."

I watched him until he disappeared into the concrete block building, which was painted a fresh, bright white. Posted on the long side were signs for restrooms and showers.

To one side of the building, light-up signs

attached to an annex with a glass front advertised food and supplies.

I watched the beach for a while, my gaze continually straying toward the group of teens. As I watched, two people stood up, brushing sand off their clothing, and waved goodbye as they headed toward a grassy picnic area behind the office building.

To my shock, I recognized them. "No way." I jumped out of the Escalade and started running, my flip flops getting bogged down in the deep yellow sand as I called out and waved. "Asher! Ame!"

The office door banged shut as I hit the grass and called again. The teens suddenly skidded to a halt, their gazes whipping in my direction a beat before they took off running.

"What the..."

"What's going on?" Hal asked, jogging up behind me.

The two kids shot away down the grassy strip on the 4-wheeler and disappeared into the woods. "Asher and Ame were here."

"Where?"

I pointed in the direction they'd gone. "They just took off on the 4-wheeler."

Hal swore softly. "I'm going to throttle him."

"What do you suppose they were doing here?"

Hal scrubbed a hand over his eyes. He looked

tired. He'd no doubt had a short and uncomfortable night on my couch. "I don't know. Let's go ask."

We turned around, and I jolted to a stop with a tiny yelp.

Mr. Pendleton stood between us and Hal's car. And he didn't look happy to see us.

I tensed, and Hal must have felt it. In a quick, subtle move, he angled himself half in front of me. "Can we help you?" he asked the other man, his voice dark with warning.

Pendleton's gaze stayed locked on mine. His expression was defiantly hostile and elusively familiar. "Why are you following me?" he asked, clearly speaking to me.

I stepped around Hal, frowning. "I believe we were here first." I nearly winced at the schoolyard overtones of my statement. A waft of "you started it!" stunk up the air between us. "But we *were* looking for you," I admitted.

Pendleton's brows lifted. He was clearly surprised by my honesty. "You don't say?"

"I do, actually." I tried a smile, but it felt tight on my lips. "Someone attacked me on my property yesterday."

"What does that have to do with me?"

"You tell us," Hal said. "Why are you in Deer Hollow?"

"That's none of your business," Pendleton

growled. "If you don't stop harassing me, I'll go to the cops."

Hal's body language remained relaxed, his voice calm. "I don't think so."

The man bristled. "Excuse me?"

"Given the fact that you're currently on parole as the result of a drug charge, I'm thinking going to the police and admitting you're mixed up in another drug investigation, with a side of murder, is probably the last thing you want to do, isn't that right, Mr. Zola?"

I sucked air in a gasp. Of course! *Pendleton...Penn.* I was an idiot! That was why he looked so familiar. Add a couple of decades and better clothes, and the man standing in front of us was the spitting image of his father, William.

"So fess up, Zola. Why are you here?" Hal prodded. His dark gaze held the other man in an unwavering grip. The tension between them was palpable. Instead of responding, the man jerked his head toward the disappearing teens on the 4-wheeler. "If you want to keep those kids safe, you'd better keep an eye on them."

Hal tensed. "Is that a threat?"

Zola's smile was hard. "Just a warning."

"Is that who you were talking about on the phone," I asked, drawing Zola's hostile attention back to me. "Are you planning to hurt the kids?"

A moment later, shrill laughter sliced through

the taut moment and we turned as a group of teens moved up behind us, laughing and teasing as they threaded their way through us and headed for the store. They filed noisily inside. The girls threw Hal an appreciative glance as they passed, and the boys glared at him with daggers in their eyes.

My PI was like a gooey Greek pastry to women of all ages. Irresistible and delicious. He just couldn't help himself.

By the time we returned our focus to Zola, he was climbing into his truck.

"Let's go," Hal said, hurrying to the car. But when we pulled out onto the highway a minute later, there was no sign of Zola.

He was already long gone.

Hal chucked a small white sticker onto the dashboard. "Dangit!"

"What's that?" I asked.

He shook his head. "The manager at the campground said we couldn't park there, even for five minutes, without a parking sticker. He apparently has a tow service on autodial."

I snorted. "How much did that cost you?"

"Five dollars." He sighed. "And we didn't even really get a chance to park."

"Chin up, Amity," I teased. "If you're nice, I'll let you bring me here after this is over. We'll just park on the road and have a picnic."

His grin turned my insides to mush. "It's a date."

The kids hadn't returned home by the time we got there. Hal tried calling Asher, but it was no surprise when he didn't answer.

Hal's phone rang as I was letting Caphy and Ethel Squeaks out the back door.

"Arno, I'm glad you called, I was going to call you." He listened for a beat and then frowned. "And nobody knows where he is?"

As I came up to him, Hal pressed the speaker button. "Arno, you're on speaker with Joey and me."

"Hey Joey," Arno said. He sounded tired. "I was just telling Hal that your counselor has disappeared. Nobody's seen him for two days."

My counselor? It took me a beat to remember who he was talking about. There was just too much going on. "Milo Dill? Could this have something to do with Medford's death?" I asked.

"Muldane's looking into that now. There's no indication Dill was involved in anything Medford was involved in. His record is clean. He got into a few minor tussles when he was drinking, but since he cleaned himself up, he's been a model citizen."

"We have a situation," Hal said. "Penn Zola's in Deer Hollow."

"Zola? Why would he be here?"

"I don't know, but with the death of Rhonda Mae

Gardner, it seems like quite a coincidence. Especially since he wouldn't tell me what he was doing in Deer Hollow."

"That is interesting."

"I heard him talking on his cell in the grocery," I told Arno. "He seemed to be threatening someone."

"And he just made a veiled threat against Asher and Ame," Hal added. "I think you should bring him in."

Arno was silent for a beat. Then he sighed. "Let me talk to your brother."

"He's not here."

"Where is he? If Zola's threatening him..."

"I'm going to find out where he is as soon as we get off the phone. And then you'll probably be arresting me for smacking him upside his thick head."

Arno chuckled. "It's times like these when I'm glad I'm an only child."

"Amen and Amen," I said with heartfelt sincerity.

The back door slammed shut, and Caphy ran full speed ahead down the hallway toward us, her muscular body wagging like a giant tail when she spotted us.

I couldn't stop a grin. My pibl always acted like she hadn't seen me in days, despite the fact that I'd just let her out into the yard two minutes earlier.

"Arno, I think the kids are back," Hal said. "I'll

call you after I talk to them." Hal disconnected, cutting off Arno's attempt to demand the first crack at Asher.

Asher came into the room, looking sheepish. Ame wasn't with him.

"Where's Ame?" I asked.

"On the porch. I told her to wait out there while you tore into me. She doesn't need to be part of that."

Hal crossed his arms over his chest. "Do you think I have a good reason to tear into you?"

Asher straightened his shoulders and looked down his perfect nose at Hal. At that moment, he looked more like his big brother than either one of them would probably like to admit. "I left the property, so yeah. But don't get all drama queen about it. It wasn't a big deal."

"It wasn't, huh?" Hal nodded, looking down at the floor. His jaw tightened, and a muscle jumped in his cheek. "Joey and I ran into Penn Zola at the campground. He all but threatened you and Ame."

I was pretty sure Asher would have continued the defiant attitude if Hal had told him Zola was only after him. But his eyes went wide when Hal included Ame. "Penn? Why? What did we do to him?"

"He's probably the one who attacked me," I told Asher.

The kid shook his dark head. The silky black

curls were messy, tousled from the wind. If possible, it made him even more adorable. "Penn wouldn't do that. I'm telling you, he's a good guy."

"Why were you at that campground?"

Asher crossed his arms over his chest. "Ame wanted to show me the lake."

"Why?"

The kid seemed to have trouble meeting his brother's eyes. "No special reason."

"Ash?"

He expelled air in a rush. "Some of Ame's friends swim there. She thought maybe somebody might know more about Rhonda Mae's death."

Hal paled. "You're asking questions about the Gardner girl's murder? Have you lost your beady little mind?"

"It's no big deal." Asher was every bit as belligerent as Hal was enraged.

"Don't you wonder why Penn just happened to be there while you and Ame were there?" Hal asked. "Did you ever consider that sticking your nose into this investigation would put a target on your back? On Ame's back?"

"That's ridiculous. You're acting like the parental units," Asher scoffed.

"I overheard Penn talking to somebody on the phone," I said. I should probably just record the recounting of my experience at Junior's and play it back for everyone. It would save time. "He certainly sounded like he was going after someone."

"What exactly did he say?" Asher demanded, earning himself a warning glare from his much bigger brother. He flushed and seemed to try to calm himself.

"He said '*he won't get a chance to tell that story*'. Do you know what that means?"

Asher paled, his gaze refusing to meet mine or Hal's.

"What aren't you telling me," Hal asked.

The kid shifted, still unable to look at us. I dropped onto the couch and let Hal and Asher hash it out. Asher's hostility toward me said he wouldn't answer any of my questions anyway.

"Meow!" LaLee sauntered past Hal and dragged her long body along Asher's ankle before jumping onto the couch and draping herself along the back.

Her action drew my gaze to Asher's feet, and alarm made my pulse spike. My gaze shot to Asher's. He frowned when he saw the look on my face. "Where did you get those shoes?" I asked.

He blinked, his frown clearing as he glanced down in surprise. "These? I don't know."

Hal stiffened when he spotted the expensive designer shoes my attacker had most likely worn that night in the woods. "Ash, please tell me you didn't attack Joey." The words emerged on a growl, his big body tensing as the full reality of Asher's culpability hit him. I don't even think he realized it when he moved closer to me.

The kid's surprise at the sudden turn of the conversation faded. Defensiveness filled his expression. "I swear I didn't attack her, Hal. I wouldn't do that."

"The person who attacked her in the woods was wearing those shoes."

The kid shrugged, but his gaze skated guiltily away.

"Take them off!" Hal demanded.

Asher blanched. "What? Why..."

"Just do it!"

The kid gave a put-upon sigh and dropped heavily into a chair. He sent me an angry glower as he tugged first one shoe, untied of course, and then the other off his feet. He tossed them to the rug at Hal's feet rather than hand them over like a civilized person.

Hal stared at the shoes on the carpet. One of them had toppled onto its side. He picked it up. The mud embedded in its tread and on the sole and toes was easy to see. Of course, it could have gotten there during Asher's romp through the woods that afternoon, but it seemed unlikely. He'd been on the 4-wheeler, not climbing ravines.

Heat suffused my face, and I looked at Hal's brother with despair. Did he hate me so much he would have hit me on the head with a tree branch? And if he did, why?

Hal's jaw tightened. His face flushed with anger. Without looking at the shoes, he leaned toward his brother. "If you touched her, I'll call Arno myself and walk you to jail."

The kid's chin jutted. "Dad won't..."

"Dad won't have anything to say about this," Hal interrupted. "You assaulted a woman on her own property." He stopped talking and clenched his teeth, his big hands fisting.

"Hal," I said softly. "I'm okay. Let's hear his side."

He took a deep, shaky breath and walked toward me. It seemed to take a monumental force of will for him to bend his legs and sit down next to me. Then he looked at Asher and said through gritted teeth. "Talk."

"What do you want me to talk about?"

Hal's jaw worked for a beat, and tension throbbed through the room. I wasn't sure if I should try to intervene.

Fortunately, Asher managed to rub a couple of brain cells together and finally realize he was in danger of being scared straight in the Deer Hollow jail. He looked down at his hands. "Okay, untwist your boxers," he told Hal. I was seriously beginning to doubt the kid's intelligence. "I was in the woods that night, but I didn't hit Joey."

The couch creaked beneath us, and I was afraid

Hal was turning to stone beside me. "What were you doing there?" he growled out.

"I went to talk to Will."

My eyebrows lifted. "Will Zola?"

Asher nodded.

"What was Will Zola doing in Joey's woods?" Hal asked.

Asher chewed his lip for a beat and then expelled air. "I told him to meet me there."

"Why?" Hal asked when Asher didn't elaborate.

"He called me, and he said he was worried about Penn. He thinks Penn's dealing again."

"Why does he think that?" I asked. Though I already had a pretty good idea why.

"He found..." Asher skimmed Hal a quick look. "There were drugs hidden in their garage."

Hal and Asher stared at each other for a long moment. Then Hal lifted a single dark eyebrow. It was as if he'd tugged a string and made Asher move. Like a virtual marionette.

The kid twitched violently. "I didn't tell you because I knew you'd think Will gave Brenda Wallace those drugs to sell. I didn't want him to go to jail."

"Of course it had nothing to do with saving your own skin," Hal growled out.

"So what if it did? You couldn't yank that stick out of your butt long enough to consider I might not be guilty. I know how you think."

"Do you?" Hal asked quietly. "Do you really? If you could ever extract yourself from being a perpetual party of one, maybe you *would* know how I think. But you can't do it, can you? You're too mired in what you want at any given moment to offer a molecule of consideration to anybody else."

"That's not fair! I was trying to help a friend."

"A friend who nearly cost Joey and Caphy their lives. A friend who's trying to protect a drug dealer and murderer. Some friend you have!" Hal yelled.

Asher shot to his feet. "Will didn't hit Joey either! He wouldn't do that."

"Then who did?"

Asher remained mulishly silent.

"Who else was in the woods that night, Asher," Hal asked, his voice quiet but firm.

"I don't know."

"Why did you run from Penn Zola today?" The quick change of subject surprised an honest response from the teen. "I don't trust him."

"Despite what Will says?" Hal asked.

"Yeah. The guy can be scary. And he has no business being here."

"Why do you think he is?" I asked.

Asher shook his head. "I don't know." When he saw Hal's expression, he opened his hands in a pleading gesture. "I promise I'm not lying, Hal. I don't know why Penn's here. But I'm pretty sure he's up to no good."

"Who was he talking about when he said '*He won't get a chance to tell that story?*'" I asked.

"I'm not sure."

"Guess," Hal ordered.

Sighing, Asher dropped into the chair. He stared at his shoeless feet for a beat. When he glanced up, there was real fear in his gaze. "I think he meant me. He doesn't trust me not to tell what I know."

"And what do you know, Ash?"

The kid looked at his brother, the fear still riding his expression. "I know Penn hung out at the recreation center a lot. I know he spent a lot of time talking to Brenda Wallace and some of the other good-time girls. I know he's been agitated since she died. He's even been mean to Will, and he's usually not."

"That's it?" Hal asked. "I'm sure lots of other people know all that too."

Asher gave him a look. "Yeah, but lots of other people don't have two Private Investigators for brothers. And lots of other people didn't just suddenly move away from Indy and into one of those PI's homes."

Light dawned, and I felt my eyes go wide. *Dangit!* By the look on Hal's face, I saw he'd realized the same thing I had.

By bringing Asher to Deer Hollow, their parents might have put a target squarely on his back.

"What about Rhonda Mae?" I asked. "Did Penn kill her too?"

I expected him to shrug off my question. Or even admit it was a possibility. But Asher paled, his eyes impossibly wide. "I'm afraid she was a warning to me. To keep my mouth shut."

17

"Muldane called me," Arno told us. "Apparently, Milo Dill told his neighbor he was going on vacation."

We were sitting on the porch, watching Ame and Asher stroll back to the house from the old hangar. Caphy danced around their feet, tongue lolling and tail manically waving. Ame had her arm through Asher's, and they looked very sweet together. I wondered if their relationship would survive a return to the big city. They were both a year away from college and almost certain separation. Something inside me hoped they stayed in touch. I liked the way Asher leaned his head close to hers when he spoke to her. And the way he tugged her gently away from Caphy when the pibl got too exuberant.

"Is it unusual for him to just leave like that?" Hal asked, drawing me back to their conversation.

"The neighbor didn't seem to think so. She said he takes a day here and there when he has a lull in his appointments."

I frowned. "A girl just died, and several of the boys who regularly visited Brighter Day Youth Center are potential suspects. It seems like a bad time for him to take off."

"I don't disagree. I'm just telling you what Muldane told me."

"I know she had doubts that Penn Zola was our guy, but I've learned some stuff that makes me wonder if he isn't in this up to his eyebrows."

"Like what?" Arno asked.

Hal glanced toward the approaching teens. "I can't get into it right now. Can I come in there and talk to you?"

"In about an hour? I haven't eaten all day. I thought I'd run out and grab something."

"Okay. I'll see you then." Hal disconnected.

I kept my voice low as the kids drew closer. "Are you going to tell him everything Asher told us?"

"Yes. If Ash is in danger, I'd like one of the Deputies to keep an eye on the house."

I grimaced but didn't disagree. "Probably makes sense." I thought about what we'd learned. The fact that Penn Zola was not only in Deer Hollow but that he might have killed Rhonda Mae as a threat to Asher was chilling. I didn't have any doubt at all that Penn was our killer. But we needed proof.

Asher threw Ethel's red ball toward the pond in the side yard and Caphy bounded after it. He and Ame took the opportunity to escape. They ran laughing to the porch and climbed the steps, breathless. "She's relentless with that ball," Asher said, laughing.

"Ethel's going to be mad you gave the pibl her new ball," I said.

"She's snoring in her tent," he told us, unapologetically. "Recharging her battery so she can torture me later, when I'm trying to sleep."

Ame giggled. "I can't believe you slept with a pig."

Asher shrugged. "She's actually pretty awesome."

"That she is," Hal agreed. He fixed Ame with a look. "Would you mind answering a few questions about Rhonda Mae?"

She gave him a hesitant smile. "If I can. I've been away for a couple of years, but I've tried to keep up with everybody."

Hal motioned to the chairs across from us. I poured the teens glasses of lemonade from the pitcher I'd brought outside. "Cookie?"

Ame shook her head, flashing Asher a look. "No, but thanks."

I remembered those days...when I didn't want boys to know I ate *anything*, let alone anything good.

She sipped her lemonade.

Asher ignored his, sitting on the edge of his

chair. One knee bounced with nervous energy.

Hal leaned forward, resting his elbows on the glass top. "What was Rhonda Mae like?"

Ame shrugged. "She seemed sweet. She wasn't really a party girl, though. I would have never expected her to sell drugs."

"You didn't know her well?"

"Not really well, no. Like most of the kids around here, we went to the same schools growing up, but she was really quiet and mostly kept to herself."

"She was shy?" I asked. I hadn't known Rhonda or her family personally. They were corn and soybean farmers and lived a few miles outside of Deer Hollow.

"Uncomfortable is a better word." Ame flushed slightly. "You know how kids are."

"They were mean to her?"

"Maybe a little. Mostly they just ignored her. The Gardners are country people. Even for this area, they were kind of backward. Rhonda Mae and her mom sewed all their own clothes, and she always brought her lunch to school." Ame shrugged. "That's not a bad thing. But it made her stand out."

"Did she have friends?" I asked, feeling my heart break a little for Rhonda Mae.

"More like acquaintances. She didn't sit alone at lunch or anything. But she never had the money to go shopping or to a show or anything, so it was probably hard for her to be social."

Hal nodded. "To your knowledge, had anybody noticed any changes in her life recently?"

Ame cocked her head. "Like what?"

"Did you or any of your friends see her talking to somebody new? Notice a change in her attitude? Or see anything that signified she might have more money than usual?"

"No. Well, Sasha Bowman did walk in on her in the girl's restroom one day after summer school. Apparently Rhonda is taking pre-college classes so she can apply the credits at IU. It will save her family a lot of money." Ame shrugged, clearly not judging, just providing information. "Sasha said Rhonda looked like she'd been crying. But when she asked her if she was okay, Rhonda had apparently insisted she was fine. She claimed she'd gotten a C on a math test. She was really smart, and she usually got As." Ame frowned. "Sash didn't believe her. She figured it had something to do with Rhonda's mom."

"Her mom?" I asked.

"Yeah. She's sick. I heard they took her to the hospital a couple of weeks ago."

Hal nodded. "How did Rhonda Mae end up at the party the other night? It doesn't sound like she usually went to them?"

"No. She didn't. I don't think I've seen her at a party since grade school. She went to Leeanne Latham's tenth birthday party and gave her a homemade dress as a gift. I thought it was pretty. I could tell somebody had spent a lot of time working on it."

The way she said it gave me the impression that somebody else hadn't appreciated the gift. My heart broke a little more. "Are there any other girls who you think might be selling drugs too? It seems unlikely Rhonda would be the only one."

Ame shook her head without hesitation. "Trust me, after what happened to poor Rhonda, I'd tell you. I don't want anybody else to die."

Hal smiled at Ame. "Thanks. You've been very helpful." He looked at me. "How about we have dinner at Sonny's. We can drop Ame off at Lis's house afterward, and then go talk to Arno."

Ame nodded, looking excited at the idea. I glanced at Asher, and he grinned. "Will there be pie?"

I laughed. "Always."

I suddenly realized that, despite a rocky start and some phenomenally poor decisions on his part, I was really starting to like the kid.

I mean, he loved pie. How bad could he be?

The bell over the door jangled as Hal pushed it open. He held it for me and I stepped into the diner. Asher tried to step through behind me, but Hal's arm snaked out and stopped him. He arched a midnight brow at his brother as Ame followed me in. She was grinning.

Sonny's was busier than usual. Most of the booths were already full of diners, and both waitresses were working. The busboy, Jimmy Boston, was clearing a table at the front and his pimply face was covered in a sheen of sweat from having to work so hard.

Max spotted me and waved. She pointed to the booth Jimmy had just cleared near the front window. I gave her a thumbs up and headed that way. Ame and I took opposite sides of the well-worn booth. We slid carefully toward the window end of the benches, taking care to avoid the cracked vinyl with our bare legs.

Max came over as Asher and Hal sat down. Loudly popping her chewing gum, she dropped menus onto the table. Max pulled a pencil from the yellow-white rat's nest on her head and poised it over a pad. "What can I get you to drink?"

No small talk. No nonsense. Right down to business. That was Max.

We gave her our drink orders and she left.

Asher glanced my way as he opened his menu. "Carb on carb crime?"

I grinned. "I'm not sure. I might do the meatloaf today."

"The meatloaf is good," Ame said, and then

flushed when Asher grinned her way. "That's what I hear, anyway."

I'd have to have a talk with that girl. She needed to be herself. Unfortunately, her role model for the perfect woman was her flawless aunt. Lis had spent her last ten years as a model existing on air and water alone. But that was no way to live.

"I'll probably have the salad," Ame said, looking unhappy with her choice.

"You can have a bite of my meatloaf I told her."

She grinned. "Thanks."

"It's nothing. We need to save room for pie, right?"

Her grin grew wider and she nodded.

"Meatloaf works for me," Hal agreed, closing his menu.

"Meatloaf it is then," Asher said, nudging Ame with his shoulder. "You can have some of mine too."

She actually giggled.

Max set our drinks down and looked at me. "What'll it be?"

"Meatloaf all around," I told Max, deliberately not looking at Ame.

Out of the corner of my eye, I saw the girl open her mouth and then close it, a secret smile curving on her pretty face.

"Got it," Max said. Instead of turning and heading for the order window, Max stepped closer and lowered her head. "Are you two investigating young Rhonda Mae's death?"

Hal nodded. "We are."

Max pursed her lips thoughtfully. I'd never seen the confident, middle-aged woman the least bit uncertain. But she suddenly seemed unsure about sharing whatever she was thinking.

"Did you know her?" I asked by way of a verbal nudge.

"I know her mama. The sweetest woman you'll ever meet." A shadow slashed through her gaze. "Pity about the cancer."

My heart broke. "I'd heard she was sick. I'm sorry it's so serious."

"Me too. That girl wouldn't get involved in anything like drugs," Max said suddenly, as if she'd had to force herself to speak the words. "Something ain't right about all that."

"I agree," I told her. "We're trying to get to the bottom of it."

"Good," Max said, jerking her head in a single nod. "Have you talked to the guy she was in the diner with?"

I felt Hal perk up. "What guy?"

Max glanced around and lowered her voice even more. "Yeah. She came in here a couple of days ago with some guy who wasn't her dad. They whispered together in one of the back booths for a while, and then he left. Rhonda Mae just sat there starin' at the table for a good twenty minutes before she left too. Something was wrong. I could tell. That man upset her."

"What did he look like?" Hal asked.

Max held her hand about six inches above her head. "Yay tall. Brown hair that ran to long. Kind eyes and a calming manner about him. He was very polite." She shook her head. "But he upset that child. Maybe he's an uncle or something. I don't know. But whatever he said to her, it upset her something awful. When he left, I saw him climb into a small red car." She frowned in thought. "I didn't get the license plate number, but there was a big dent in the front bumper."

The bell over the door jangled again, and we all turned that way.

Arno stood in front of it, his handsome face grim. He spotted us and strode over.

"I'll put your order in," Max said, heading for the kitchen.

Hal slid out of the booth and shook Arno's hand. "Still haven't eaten?" He grinned at the cop.

Arno sighed. "Detective Muldane called again. I've been on the phone with her for a half-hour."

"News on the case?"

"Yeah. She went over to Dill's home and discovered it had been ransacked." He frowned. "Dill had one of those camera doorbells and Brita was able to access the footage." Arno fixed Hal with a look that spoke volumes. "Someone we know went into Dill's home."

I didn't need Arno to tell me who it was.

"You're sure it was him?" Hal asked. Apparently, he didn't need the cop to tell him either.

"Ninety percent. He was wearing a hoodie and kept his face averted. But the jaw looked right and the height and build. I'd stake my reputation on it."

Penn Zola.

Arno glanced at the teens across the booth. "Join me at my table when you're done, and I'll fill you in."

"So much for staying out of the investigation," I murmured to Hal as Arno strode away.

He sighed, his gaze skimming quickly to Asher.

The two teens had their heads together and they were talking softly, lost in their own little world.

"Yeah. It seems that his investigation and ours are mingling together."

"What do you make of Max's story," I asked Hal.

He frowned. "I'm not sure what to make of it. Penn Zola doesn't have long hair."

"Or kind eyes," I said, grimacing.

Our food arrived. We fell silent as Max handed the four enormous plates of meatloaf, mashed potatoes and gravy, and green beans with chunks of ham around the table.

Then nobody spoke at all for several minutes. We were too busy devouring the delicious food.

18

Asher drove Ame home in Hal's Escalade and I joined Arno and Hal for the debrief. Unfortunately, my phone rang as I was sitting down and I saw it was Reverend Smythe. I excused myself and headed outside the diner to take the call. "Hello, Pastor."

"Joey, I'm so glad I reached you." He sounded excited.

"Is everything okay?"

"Yes, yes, of course. I'm only calling because you were asking me about Milo Dill."

"The counselor in Indy, yes."

"Right. I wanted to tell you, I actually ran into Milo today. Turns out he's been here for a few days. He's on a working vacation. I believe he came to offer the student I recommended that sponsorship."

I felt my pulse speed. "Milo Dill is here in Deer Hollow?"

The reverend chuckled. "Small world, eh? He says he enjoys this area and comes here whenever he gets a chance. It's close enough to Indy that he doesn't waste half his time in the car, and he finds the river and the bluffs invigorating."

"That's great. Hal and I wanted to speak to him." More importantly, since Dill came to us, Detective Muldane would have a harder time blaming us for talking to him. Win-win. "Do you know where he's staying?"

"I'm afraid not. He was in a hurry and we didn't get much of a chance to chat. But I did get his cell phone number. Would you like that? I'm sure if you called him he'd be happy to help. He's very dedicated to his job."

"Thanks. That would be great." I punched the phone number he gave me into my phone. "Thanks so much, Reverend Smythe."

"It's no bother at all, Joey. Good luck with your investigation."

I disconnected the call and immediately dialed Dill's number. The phone rang several times and then dumped me into voice mail. I left Dill a message asking him to call and then returned to the table.

Hal looked up as I slid in next to him. "That was

Reverend Smythe. He said Milo Dill is in Deer Hollow. He's apparently been here a few days."

Hal frowned.

"What?" I asked.

"Penn Zola and this counselor are both in Deer Hollow when another girl dies. That's just too much of a coincidence for me."

Arno held Hal's gaze. "Don't forget your brother," he pointed out, lifting a hand when Hal bristled. "That's not an accusation," he said quickly. "I don't believe Asher had anything to do with the girl's death. But as you said, three people who were in the orbit of the Brenda Wallace murder in Indianapolis are here in Deer Hollow when another girl dies under the same circumstances..." He shook his head. "That stretches credulity."

Yes, it did.

Arno's phone rang. He sighed and answered. "Deputy Willager." He listened for a moment and then slid a glance toward Hal. "He's here with me now." A beat later, his features sharpened. "We'll be right there." Arno was already sliding out of the booth as he disconnected. "You need to come with me to the hospital."

We started moving.

"Why? What's happened?" Hal asked.

Arno started toward the door. "There's been an accident. Asher's been hurt."

I sat in a small waiting room in Emergency, my nerves jangling. Every time someone in scrubs walked down the hallway, I had to force myself to stay seated. I just wanted to grab somebody and shake them until Asher's condition fell out of them.

I checked my phone again for about the hundredth time. I'd left Lis a message as we'd raced to the hospital, and she hadn't responded yet.

My greatest fear, after hearing that Asher was critically injured, was that Lis and Ame had gotten caught up in whatever was going on. What if Penn had done something to them? It wasn't like my best friend to ignore my calls. Not for the first time, I wished I had Ame's cell number.

If only I could get hold of Asher's phone, I could get it from that.

But Asher's phone was probably in a bag of his belongings in the emergency room. *Please, God*, I prayed silently. *Let him be okay*. The unthinking, desperate plea to a higher power brought Reverend Smythe's urgings back to me. I suddenly understood why he kept prompting me to come to church. It was comforting to know that there was a higher power who could stand in your corner. The most terrifying thing about feeling alone was the helplessness. If you're alone and you need a miracle, you're destined for sorrow.

Footsteps sounded on the hallway floor again, and my head came up. Arno's expression looked dire, his usual intensity replaced by a worried look that made my pulse spike. I jumped to my feet and hurried over to him. "Please tell me he's okay?"

Arno took my arm and led me back to my chair, giving me a nudge. "Sit."

I locked my knees. "I don't want to sit. I want to know that Asher's okay."

Arno sat, scrubbing a hand over his face. His palm scraped over a golden crop of bristles that gave him a roguish air. He sighed wearily. "The doctors won't let me in the room. I don't know any more than you do."

His admission tugged the starch from my knees, and I fell back into my chair. "I feel like I'm going to explode if I don't hear soon."

Arno reached over and squeezed my hand. "Take deep breaths."

"I've already tried that. I nearly passed out."

His lips curved.

I threw myself back in the chair, trying not to think about how Hal was going to feel if his brother was...

Nope. Not even thinking it. Desperate for another topic to distract me, I looked at Arno. "Have you spoken to Lis lately?"

His head came up, and his brown eyes narrowed. "No. Why?"

"She's not returning my calls or texts. I'm starting to worry."

He grabbed his phone and dialed. As the phone continued to ring without being answered, the worry on his face turned into alarm. He stood. "I'm going to her house."

I wanted to jump up and go with him, but I couldn't. "You'll let me know if..." I gave my head a little shake. "*When* you find her?"

Arno grunted in what I took as an affirmative and hurried out of the room.

I gave up trying to sit and started to pace. I'd patrolled the equivalent of a marathon by the time I heard Hal's familiar stride eating up the hallway, heading in my direction.

One look at his handsome, weary face had me sobbing. He grabbed me up and kissed my temple. "He's going to be fine."

Thank you, I whispered to the entity I'd begged for a miracle. "I've been so worried."

Hal's muscles flexed beneath my cheek as he nodded. "He has a broken leg, some bruised ribs, and his perfect nose is slightly crooked. He's going to look like a prizefighter."

I gave a watery laugh. "The girls will love it."

Hal sighed, his arms still tightly wrapped around me. After a moment, he pulled back. "I called mom and dad."

I scrubbed tears off my face, sniffling. "Are they coming down?"

He nodded.

Then I remembered my newest fear. "Arno's heading to Lis's house to check on her and Ame."

Hal frowned. "Is there a problem?"

"I don't know. Lis isn't responding to my calls or texts. I don't have Ame's number, so I can't call her."

Hal reached into his pocket and pulled out Asher's phone. I recognized it because the case had a serious-looking rubber bumper. He quickly scanned through his brother's recents and tapped a number. The phone rang several times before he disconnected. "She's not answering either." His frown deepened. "This isn't good."

No, it wasn't. "Penn has them."

"Don't jump to conclusions, honey." Hal pulled out his own phone and dialed again. "Are they there?" he asked whoever he'd called. I presumed it was Arno. Hal listened, nodding a couple of times, and then frowned. "What did she say?"

Relief filled me. Arno must have gotten in touch with Lis.

Hal swore softly. "Okay, we'll go out there now." He disconnected and looked at me. "Lis's nosy neighbor saw a truck near her house that could have been Penn Zola's pickup." He grimaced. "Or one of a hundred other trucks around Deer Hollow. It's probably nothing, but bears looking into. Feel like going back to that campground?"

"Please! I can't sit here for another minute."

It wasn't until we were standing out on the sidewalk that we remembered we had no car. Hal's Escalade had been towed to The Greasy Wrench after Asher was run off the road.

Hal expelled a frustrated breath.

"I'll call a cab," I told him, giving him a supportive nudge with my shoulder.

Twenty minutes later, we were climbing into my Jeep with Caphy bouncing happily in the back seat. We hadn't intended to bring her, but in the end, she took the decision out of our hands. She'd danced away as I grabbed for her and jumped through the car door Hal was holding open for me. I hadn't had the heart to drag her back out again. She was so excited.

I let Hal drive because I thought he needed something to do more than I did. As he pulled out onto Goat's Hollow Road, Caphy gave each of us a happy wet willie and then settled back to stare out the back window and smear it up with her nose.

We headed toward the campground, which was only a mile away from my house as the crow flies, the property backing up to my hundred acres.

It took us three minutes to make the trip.

"What are we looking for?" I asked Hal as he

turned into the campground. He drove past the office/shower/store building.

"Asher got a glimpse of the car that rammed him." His gaze found mine. "He described Zola's pickup truck."

I felt my eyes go wide. "And you think it will be here?"

Hal's gaze had been skimming the vehicles parked with the campers as he drove slowly through the grounds. The campground was even more populated than the last time we'd been there. Apparently, the camping thing was popular around Deer Hollow.

My gaze skimmed the cars too, though I had no idea what I was looking for. Until I saw it. "Hey, could that be Milo Dill's car?" The little red car with the big dent in the bumper sat beneath the white glow of a light pole.

Hal slowed to a stop behind the car. He cut the engine. "Let's talk to him. He might know where Zola is."

I climbed out and followed Hal toward the camper. He stopped beside the little red car and peeked inside, testing the door and finding it locked. I stood in the warm night, peering around. A warm yellow glow filled the windows of some of the trailers, gilding the movements of the campers shifting past windows and creating shadows behind curtains. The family directly across from us sat around a firepit in folding chairs, the kids happily roasting marshmallows in a briskly dancing fire. The smell of the fire wafted in our direction, and a wave of nostalgia slid over me. When I was a kid, my family had liked to make s'mores over a pretty campfire. The memory was bittersweet, and I decided in that moment I wanted to capture it again. Part of moving into the next phase of my life was embracing the old with the new. Losing my parents had torn possibilities from my life. But that severing of old experiences didn't have to be permanent.

My eyes burned with sudden tears. I scraped the moisture away with the heels of my hands as Hal wrapped an arm around my shoulders. "You okay?"

I nodded. "I just got some smoke in my eyes." Caphy started to bark, her muscular body slamming against the car door until I was afraid she was going to hurt herself. "Caphy!" I called, using my sternest tone. She ignored me and kept throwing herself against the window.

"Your windows are going to be trashed," Hal said as he reached up to knock on the metal door of the old-fashioned, truck camper.

I sighed.

"Mommy, look at the pwetty puppy!" The little girl across the street had deserted her roasting marshmallow and slipped off her chair. Her gaze transfixed on the excited dog inside my trembling car, she ambled toward Caphy as if in a trance.

"Oh, oh."

Hal knocked again and reached for the knob, finding the camper unlocked. "You go deal with that. I don't think Dill's here. I'll just give this place a quick look, and we'll hit the road again."

I nodded, hurrying back to the car as the little boy joined the tiny girl. "Hi!" I said, giving the kids a smile.

The father stood in the road, unsure if he should stop them.

I gave him a wave. "It's okay. She's friendly."

He nodded and smiled.

"Your puppy is pwetty," the little girl said.

Caphy stopped flinging herself at the door and stared through the window at her visitors, whining with excitement. She loved kids. Adored them. To her, being loved on by a small human was the equivalent of three dog cookies. "Thank you," I said. "Would you like to pet her?"

"Yeth, pwease."

The little girl pushed a long, shiny lock of wavy blonde hair behind her ear. Her brother, who looked to be a couple of years older than her, was trying to look wise and indifferent. But I saw the way his eyes lit up when he looked at Caphy.

"I'll get her out so you can see her."

I carefully cracked the passenger side door and reached into the glove compartment, tugging out a leash. Caphy indulged me by jumping into the front seat and letting me clip the leash onto her collar. When I opened the door, she leaped out, happily scrubbing my knee with her wet tongue before giving me an excited bark. "That's a pretty girl. You need to be gentle, okay?"

We'd been working on gentle. I was convinced Caphy understood the concept, but her natural exuberance sometimes overwhelmed her training. However, she was a perfect little princess as I led her around the car and stopped, allowing the kids to come over and see her.

Her tail whacked my leg as they approached. Her wide pink tongue lolled.

"Sit," I told her.

Caphy sat, her whole body vibrating with excitement.

The little girl petted her on the nose. "Hewwo, pwetty puppy."

Caphy scraped her tongue over the little girl's face, and the toddler giggled happily.

Her brother moved in and pressed himself against Caphy's side. He rested his cheek against her squishy head. It was so sweet.

"Gentle," I reminded her as she vibrated. She sat as still as she was able for about a minute and then she stuck her tongue in the little boy's ear.

He erupted into giggles. "He kissed my ear!"

Caphy jumped up and went into a playful position, butt up, tail manically wagging.

The father joined his kids and scratched my happy dog under the chin. "She's beautiful," he said. "We want to get a dog. We've been waiting until the kids get older. More for the dog's sake than theirs."

I laughed with him. "She's my best friend."

He nodded. "Come on, kids. Let's let this nice lady get back to her visit."

Caphy whined as the kids started to walk away. The little girl ran back and wrapped her tiny arms around my dog's neck, kissing her on the cheek. "Bye, puppy."

Caphy slobbered on the toddler's face again, sending her off on a happy giggle.

I watched them go and turned, wondering what was taking Hal so long.

The door to Dill's trailer suddenly flew open, and a man clambered clumsily down the steps, his knees nearly buckling as he stepped into the thick grass.

I watched in confusion as he ran toward us. Too late, I realized he was going to barrel right into Caphy and me. Before I could react, he'd shoved me to the side and Caphy was on him, growling and tugging him away from me.

Hal bolted from the camper, looking alarmed. He yelled my name as the man who was fighting my dog somehow managed to break free and throw himself into my Jeep.

I watched in horror as Penn Zola took off in my

car, whipping it around in an empty slot and tearing past us up the road.

I barely caught Caphy's leash before she started to take off after him.

Hal had his phone out. "Are you okay?"

I nodded, brushing rocks from my knees. "What just happened?" I asked as Arno's voice came on the line.

Hal held up a finger to silence me. "Arno, we have a problem."

19

"Has Arno found Lis and Ame?" I shifted in the cloth seat, hearing a telltale crunching sound under my jeans. Slipping my hand underneath a butt cheek, I dug around for the offending item. I'd been trying to clear all the debris from the seat since the nice family across from Dill's had offered us the use of their minivan.

Caphy whined unhappily. She'd been watching me dig for gold in the seat and had probably been hoping I'd send whatever I found her way. But, from the way she'd been snuffling around the child's car seat in the back, I was pretty sure she'd already gotten a meal's worth of crumbs.

"Not yet." Hal skimmed me a look. "What's going on over there?"

I grimaced. "I'm pretty sure somebody dumped an entire bag of chips on this seat." Reaching under my left buttock, I extracted a thick, yellow shard. I was pretty sure it had petrified. "Corn chips by the look of it."

I threw the shard onto the floor, where it got lost in a chaos of stuff that included a lot of fast-food wrappers, a pair of worn white sneakers in a woman's size, a hairbrush, a pile of used tissues, and something fuzzy I was afraid to examine too closely.

My nose wrinkled. "It smells like butt in here."

Hal didn't chuckle. In fact, his intensity was making my skin itch. "What do you think is going on?"

"I think somebody needs to clean out this car," he responded without humor.

"No, I mean with this case."

Hal entered Deer Hollow proper and slowed to a crawl. His gaze swiveled from one side of Main street to the other, searching for Penn and my Jeep. "From the condition of Dill's camper, I'm guessing he and Penn fought, and Dill took off with Penn's truck."

"So it was Dill's camper?" I asked, surprised.

"Dill's laptop and wallet were on the table so that's my guess."

"Where was Penn when you went inside?"

"I didn't see him until he bolted for the door. I think he was probably in the bed at the front, behind a curtain."

"Why would Dill take Penn's truck? His car was there."

"Probably the same reason Penn took your Jeep. It was parked behind his car."

I nodded. The simplest answer was usually the right one. "Why would Penn attack Dill?"

"I've been thinking about that," Hal responded, gaze still skimming the street, "I'm wondering if maybe Dill was his target all along. Maybe he wasn't after Asher."

"Then who attacked me in the woods? And why? And what about poor Rhonda Mae?"

"We know the girl talked to somebody at the diner who wasn't Zola. Maybe Dill was investigating what was going on with the kids. Maybe he somehow learned the person enticing these girls to sell drugs had moved his operation to Deer Hollow."

"That makes sense, I guess."

He slid me a look. "You don't sound convinced."

I shrugged. "That still doesn't explain who hit me on the head in the woods."

"No. It doesn't."

We eased along Main Street, the big sign for Brats versus Broads just ahead of us on my side of the street. As we moved slowly past, the street light glinted off of something near the back of the lot. I jolted with recognition. "Stop!"

Hal eased the minivan to a stop at the curb. "What did you see?"

I twisted around in my seat, trying to see behind the building. Unfortunately, the enormous sign for the daycare blocked that whole end of the building from view. "I thought I saw my Jeep."

Hal turned off the car, pocketing the keys. "You and Caphy stay here."

I opened the door, reaching for Caphy's leash. "Not a chance, bud."

He sighed and grabbed the leash from me as I stepped down into the moist grass. A moment later, Caphy was outside the car. She'd stopped for a beat to snuffle my seat, looking for crumbly remains.

I winced as my flip flops took on enough water to make me slip and slide like an inebriated party girl.

Apparently, the daycare had a sprinkler system —just my luck.

Hal handed the leash back to me. "Ready?"

I nodded. He took off at a jog, and Caphy surged after him. I jogged too, for about two strides, and then my foot slipped sideways, falling out of my flip flop, and I went down in the wet grass. As I splashed down, water sprayed upward, bathing my face and hair.

"Dangit!" I mumbled softly.

Hal stopped and turned just as Caphy decided she *really needed* to keep moving. The pibl took off, digging into the grass and tugging me behind her like a Musher without a sled. "Caphy, no!" I growled out. She stopped but gave me an impatient bark to let me know I was cramping her style.

Hal jogged back. "It would be faster if you stayed

on your feet," he said, his luscious lips curving with humor.

"Har," I told him, climbing to my hands and knees.

He gave me a hand up. His palm slipped from my wet grip as I stood and the sudden loss of support nearly sent me sprawling again.

Stumbling a couple of steps, I steadied. Then I looked down and grimaced. I was soaked.

"You sure you don't want to wait in the car?"

I gave Hal a quelling look and pulled off my flip flops. "Let's go, funny man."

I'd been right. My Jeep was parked in the employee lot at the back of the building. Penn hadn't bothered to drive into a spot. He'd just stopped driving and climbed out of it, leaving the door open and the keys dangling in the ignition.

Penn Zola's truck was parked in front of a short concrete sidewalk that led to the back door of the daycare.

Hal tugged the keys from my jeep and checked the truck for keys. Finding none, he placed my keys behind a decorative rock and motioned for me to stay where I was.

His phone vibrated in his pocket. He tugged it out and eyed the screen, poking the button to answer it. "Arno? I think we found Zola..." He went very still and stiffened.

Watching his expression grow cold, I had a

horrible feeling. Hal's jaw tightened. He glanced at me. "I understand." He disconnected.

"Did he find Lis?" When Hal didn't respond, my dread-filled instincts sharpened. "Is it Asher? Is he okay?"

Hal suddenly jolted into movement. He went over to the rock and retrieved my keys, shoving them at me. "Go. Get out of here. Take Caphy."

I pushed the keys back at him. "No. Tell me what's going on."

He shook his head, grabbed the door of the Jeep and wrenched it open. "Caphy, come!"

My dog looked at Hal, a man she adored almost as much as she loved me. She whined softly, her tail giving a single, disheartened wag. Then she moved closer to me, pressing against my leg.

We both stared at Hal. "Tell me," I demanded.

"There's no time..."

"Hal."

"A jogger in Lis's neighborhood waved at Lis as she rode by in a pickup truck. The man said Lis didn't look happy and mouthed something that could have been 'Help'. He shook it off at the time, figuring he'd been imagining things, until he spotted Arno's radio car in her driveway a few minutes ago. Arno's still interviewing him, but..." Hal shook his head. "The jogger thought he saw a second figure in the backseat."

Ame!

"Did he get a look at the driver?" I asked.

"No. But the description of the truck definitely matched Penn's." Hal and I slowly turned to the truck sitting next to the Jeep.

"Dangit!" I gripped Caphy's leash with suddenly sweaty hands.

Hal nodded, shoving the keys at me again. "Go. I want to know you're safe."

"Aw, isn't this sweet?" a voice said from the shadows near the daycare building.

Hal moved to stand between the man coming out of the darkness at the side of the lot and me. The man held a gun on us, and his strides were sure, his manner aggressive.

"He's trying to protect you, Joey," the man with the gun said. "But that's not going to be possible, I'm afraid."

The man's voice was familiar. It held strains of one I'd heard on the other side of a grocery aisle. But it wasn't Penn.

His face was hidden inside a hoodie, but the quality sweatpants and expensive sneakers told me I was dealing with an older man—a man who was used to things going according to plan. Though I wasn't sure exactly how he'd expected the current mess to have gone down, I was pretty sure it hadn't gone the way he'd wanted. The tightness in the bristled jawline was all the proof I needed of that.

"Zola," Hal said, his hand moving to calm Caphy as she started to growl.

William Zola smiled, finally walking into the illumination provided by the security light high above our heads. "We meet again, Mr. Amity. How's your baby brother?"

Hal's big hands fisted. "You know how he is, Zola. Your son tried to kill him."

Zola cocked his head. "Did he? How strange." His smile was mean. Something sparked in his gaze as if he held a terrible secret he really wanted to share.

We needed to stall for time. Surely Arno would find us. Maybe one of his deputies would drive by and see us standing there. Maybe one of the neighbors would look out a window. "Why did you attack me in the woods?" I asked. I could stall. It was what I did best. Well, that and eating carbs. I was pretty spectacular at that too.

Zola nodded as if agreeing with my question. I was starting to wonder if the man was truly mad. "Yes, that. Ugly business. Unfortunately, it couldn't be helped. I couldn't have you walking around. Not with what you know."

"I don't know anything. I have no idea what you're talking about."

His expression turned cruel. "Don't lie to me!"

I jumped slightly at the tone. Caphy's growl turned to a snarl. She pressed more tightly against my leg. Between her and Hal, I was starting to feel like the middle crayon in the box. I tried to elbow Hal away, but he stuck to my side like glue. If Zola was going to shoot me, I didn't want him or my dog to get in the way. "Hal," I muttered softly.

He just shook his head, angling his body closer as if he intended to take the bullet himself.

Fear dragged icy claws along my spine and I shivered.

Or, maybe it was the fact that I was soaking wet. It definitely could have been that.

"What do you think I know?" I tried again. I was happy to stand there until the police showed up.

Zola barked out a harsh laugh. "Nice try." He jerked the gun toward the Jeep. "Put the dog in the car, Amity."

Hal didn't move. Caphy leaped forward, spittle flying away from her snarling muzzle.

Zola repositioned his gun downward. He was going to shoot my dog!

"No!" I moved in front of Caphy, hands up. "I'll put her in the car."

"Do it then. Now!" the man growled.

"Caphy!" I ordered, catching her attention. "Be still, girl."

She stopped snarling but returned her deadly gaze to Zola. A low growl still vibrated in her chest. I led her toward my Jeep and she jumped in, tail wagging. She clearly thought we were going to make our escape. Tears burned my eyes. I wrapped my arms around her neck and kissed her squishy face. "I love you, sweet girl."

I closed the door but didn't latch it. If something happened to me, I wanted Caphy to be able to get out of the car. I didn't want her trapped.

I stepped away from the Jeep and Hal moved me gently behind him.

Zola motioned toward the building. "Inside. Now."

I t was strange coming into the daycare through the kitchen at the back. Instead of the mounds of toys and long tables of blonde wood covered in crayon drawings, I was looking at a small space with a refrigerator, a short counter with a sink, and a stainless steel stove that had been meticulously scoured. The length of the outside wall was lined with a cubby cabinet, which I imagined would be filled with lunch pails and medications if the daycare were open. Each cubby had a small card clipped to it with a child's name clearly marked, and instructions that were too small to read from the door. We stood in a short hallway. There were two family-style restrooms across the hall from the kitchen, doors open and lights off.

The light from the kitchen was enough to show

me a rocking chair in each room, along with a changing table and kid-sized sink and toilet.

Between the two rooms, covering most of the wall, was a duplicate of the scene depicted on the massive sign outside.

I didn't smile at the baby bottle shooting lightning bolts. I wasn't finding anything funny at the moment.

Hal's hand was warm in the small of my back. His big form felt comforting behind me. Until I realized that protective bulk would be a perfect target for the gun Zola was holding.

The hallway was too narrow for me to maneuver around behind him. Not that he'd let me. But I moved quickly toward open space ahead, hoping the threat to Hal would be reduced if we had more room to move and react.

We emerged into the main playroom at the front of the building. The light was minimal, confined to a set of recessed step lights set low in the walls. I heard a soft noise when we came into the room, but when I glanced in the direction of the sound, I only saw what looked like a pile of stuffed animals in the shadows.

Motion out of the corner of my eye had me turning toward the front door, which was separated from the rest of the room by a short, low wall.

A man stood behind the wall, his head tipped with surprise. "Who are these people, Zola?"

I didn't recognize the man's voice, but I was pretty sure I knew who it was. "Milo Dill?" I asked.

The man turned to me. "Do I know you?"

"No," Hal said. "But, unfortunately, you knew Brenda Wallace and Rhonda Mae Gardner, didn't you?"

Dill turned toward Zola. "Have you been telling tales?"

Zola shrugged. "I told you to get rid of her. She talked to Medford."

Dill nodded. He stepped closer, stopping in front of a step light. I blinked when I saw the familiar sneakers on his feet.

"Those are pretty expensive shoes for a youth counselor," I said.

Dill blinked and looked down as if he'd forgotten what shoes he had on. "Oh, yes. They're a bit gaudy, actually. But when one works with kids, it helps to enter their world." He smiled at Zola. "Old Bill over there is very generous with the goodies. Aren't you Bill?"

Zola tensed, the gun dropping slightly as Dill pulled his attention away. "Don't call me that."

Dill laughed. "That's right. You prefer William, don't you? It sounds much snootier."

Zola's gun hand lowered some more. "Let's put our issues on the back burner for now, Dill. We have a problem we need to deal with."

Dill slid a shadowed gaze over us. "Yes. We certainly do. That was more of your handiwork."

"Shut up!" Zola barked out, the gun he was holding sliding toward Dill. "This is just as much your fault as mine. If you hadn't killed that girl in Indy we wouldn't be in this position now. Everything was coming along nicely."

I slid my gaze to Hal, and he nodded. His posture relaxed slightly, and he eased closer to Zola without seeming to move. For a big guy, my PI could be very stealthy when he set his mind to it.

Since Dill seemed very good at getting under Zola's skin, I decided it would be a good idea to keep Dill going. I looked at him. "Why did you kill Brenda Wallace?"

His stare stayed locked on Zola's face. He didn't even glance at the gun that was pointing his way. Milo Dill was a very cool customer. "The girl was stupid. She shouldn't have gone to Medford." He sniffed. "She didn't think I knew. Thought she was so smart. But I have spies everywhere." He laughed. "Everybody loves a youth counselor, and nobody suspects us of anything."

He was wrong. Hal and I were currently suspecting him of a lot of things. None of it good.

"Medford? You mean Garland Medford?"

Zola's gaze jerked my way. "Don't pretend you don't already know. Medford came to you. He's already told you about our little organization."

"He didn't tell me anything except to stay out of it."

Dill snorted out a laugh. "If that's the truth, which I highly doubt, you don't listen very well."

I shrugged. He wasn't wrong.

I caught movement out of the corner of my eye, and half turned toward it. The daycare office was set on the same wall as the kitchen. The office took up the front part of the building on one side, and the small kitchen took up the rest. I stared at the frosted glass in the door for a moment but didn't see anything moving behind it.

False alarm. I had apparently imagined the movement.

"So why did you come to Deer Hollow?" I asked the two men. "You didn't have enough of a drug market in Indianapolis?"

Hal shifted sideways and he was suddenly three inches farther away than before. I hadn't even seen him move. Zola's distrusting gaze locked on my PI and held for a beat, narrowing.

Hal crossed his arms, looking bored.

Unfortunately, Zola wasn't buying it. He shifted the gun back in our direction. But Hal's new position meant he couldn't point it at both of us at the same time. He opened his mouth, probably to tell Hal to move back, but Dill cut him off.

"There's too much competition in the city. That's why we were focusing on the Brown County area.

But our plan was always to expand all the way to the Kentucky line. Everybody knows you bumpkins love drugs. You're always cooking up your own." He grinned widely. "I'm just here to make your lives simpler. No muss, no fuss, and totally non-threatening."

"Is that why you used young girls?" I asked. My lip curled with disgust despite my best efforts.

"Of course! Who could be afraid of a sweet little thing? The drugs practically sell themselves. And the girls don't tend to get ideas about stabbing me in the back. They're much easier to control."

"All evidence to the contrary," a familiar voice said from the corner. My head whipped around. My vision had adjusted to the low light since we'd come into the room. I could see Lis among the stuffed toys. She flung something away from her, probably the gag that had kept her from talking up to that point, and reached over to tug the tape from Ame's mouth.

Zola's gun swung in their direction. I made a small, panicked sound and moved, putting myself between the gun and the two women. "No!" I yelled, flinging up my hands as Zola aimed.

20

Hal kicked out and his foot connected with Zola's knee, buckling his leg on a scream of pain. The shot went high, ripping a hole into the ceiling as Zola fought to regain his balance.

The sound of the shot was painful in the enclosed space, as was the second explosion that fractured the wall an inch from Hal. With a horrified shout, I realized Dill had pulled a gun and was shooting at my PI.

"Hal!" I screamed, looking around for something to use as a weapon.

To my horror, Hal threw himself on top of me, and we hit the floor as Dill got off a second shot.

Almost as soon as he hit the floor, Hal was up and running, crouched low.

I started to turn to see what Dill was up to, but a movement to my left clawed my attention back to

Zola. He was back on his feet and he had his weapon up. It was pointing at Hal.

"Here!" Lis shouted. I turned as she tossed something in my direction, my hand coming up to catch the hard plastic sword she threw me.

I shoved to my feet. With the hard little sword held out in front of me, I threw myself at Zola, stabbing the sword as hard as I could into his middle.

I hit him hard, the momentum of my rush giving the toy extra stopping power. He screamed in pain, really feeling my strike. It might have been the fact that I hit a bit south of where I'd been aiming.

Zola doubled over, a horrible screech emerging from between his lips.

He dropped the gun and I kicked it out of his reach.

Lis and Ame joined me, looking pale and scared but otherwise unharmed. "Are you okay?" my BFF asked. My answer was to wrap her in a bone-crunching hug.

She patted my hand, gasping out, "Uncle!"

"Who's that guy?" Ame asked, drawing our attention to the spot by the front door where Hal stood talking to another guy. Milo Dill lay on the floor between them, unmoving.

My eyes went wide. "Penn Zola?" I started forward.

The floor behind me creaked.

I started to turn.

The world exploded into motion in the form of a muscular blonde demon with angry green eyes. Caphy slammed into the man who'd been sneaking up on me. Her heavy body taking Zola down to the floor hard.

The man was tougher than he looked. But my pibl was more than he'd bargained for.

Zola screamed as he fought to avoid Caphy's snarling teeth. The hand that was again clutching the gun — dangit! — was waving dangerously around my dog as Zola tried to hit her with the weapon.

Ame was suddenly standing next to him. She cocked her leg and kicked Zola's flailing arm with everything she had. The girl had quite a kick. I vaguely remembered Lis telling me she'd been the kicker on her soccer team at school.

The man's screams took on a new urgency as the bone in his wrist cracked, and the gun flew across the room. "Girls don't give you any trouble, huh?" Ame crossed her arms over her chest and glared down at the shrieking man. "That's for Rhonda Mae, you scum bucket."

Undeterred by all the shrieking, Caphy stood on Zola's chest, her snarling muzzle mere inches from his face.

Hal walked over and looked down at him. "Good girl, Caphy. Leave it."

Caphy gave her muscular tail a quick wag,

whined softly as if to say, "Do I really have to?" and then stepped back, bouncing happily back to me.

Ame burst into tears and let herself be led away by Lis.

Someone shouted near the back of the building. Hal's head came up. "In here, Arno." He'd already flipped Zola over and zip-tied his wrists behind him, amid much pain-filled cursing.

"Where'd you get the zip ties?" I asked.

Hal grinned, pointing to the Art area, which consisted of several baskets of arts and crafts supplies in a large cabinet under the big front window. "I'm crafty."

I snorted out a laugh. "Those were probably left-over from when Billy Rogers was hauled away at three and a half to serve his first term for assault."

Hal grimaced, folding in on himself a bit at the memory.

Billy Rogers was a toddler who'd assaulted Hal with a plastic gun when we'd come to the daycare to question a witness on our very first case together.

I held up the sword. "If it makes you feel any better, I did a Billy Rogers on Zola with this."

Hal eyed the sword, his lips twitching with a grin he was trying to restrain. "Respect."

I laughed. But as Arno walked over to Penn Zola and shook his hand, I felt as if the world had stopped turning, and we'd all fallen into the rabbit hole. "What's going on over there?"

Two of Arno's fellow deputies were hauling Dill to his feet and dragging him outside. Two more were gathering Zola up.

I was pleased to see that Zola was still a bit green around the gills. I couldn't resist brandishing my weapon one last time, enjoying the moment when he flinched.

"Turns out Penn Zola isn't what we thought," Hal was saying when I refocused on him. "He was working with the IMPD to catch the person behind the drugs and the murders. He suspected his dad had an accomplice, but he didn't put the pieces together until one of the kids told him they'd seen Dill talking to Brenda Wallace the night she was killed."

So Will and Asher had been right. Penn had been trying to help the kids. I watched them haul Dill out. "What's with those ugly shoes? How many of our suspects have them? And why didn't the purchases show up on Arno's search?"

"Penn told me Will had given them out to some of his best friends. Apparently, William Zola got several pairs from a client for whom he'd developed custom software."

"Looks like Dill got a pair too."

Hal nodded. "He wasn't lying—psychology 101. Kids trust adults who understand their culture. Milo Dill was apparently very good at pretending he understood them." Grimacing, Hal said, "It's a shame. He should have been the person they could trust almost as much as their parents. In some cases, more. What he did was a huge betrayal."

"So Zola and Dill didn't know Penn was here? How is that possible? Zola didn't even react to seeing Penn's truck in the lot."

"Because he knew Dill had driven it over. I'm guessing the problem with Penn's interference was one of the 'issues' Zola referred to that he and Dill needed to deal with later."

"Who drove my Jeep over? I could have sworn it was Penn who jumped into it at the campground."

Hal nodded. "It was. William Zola was dropped off here by his driver when Dill called to tell him he had Lis and Ame here. He probably didn't want anybody to ID his car at the place, in case he ended up cleaning house. Dill and William were planning to use Lis and Ame to draw you in. But, as luck would have it, you brought yourself here." He grimaced.

"Okay, but that still doesn't answer my question. If Penn drove the Jeep, how is it possible his dad didn't know he was here?"

Arno lifted the keys, smiling at me. "William Penn assumed *we'd* come in the Jeep. The van is out of sight from the parking lot."

Arno, Lis, and Ame joined us. Arno's fingers were twined tightly with Lis's. It made me want to smile. They were so cute together. "I'm taking Lis and Ame home," Arno said. "Do you need anything from me before we go?"

"Yeah, try to get someone to admit to attacking me," I told him. "I'll feel better when I know the guy's in jail."

"Sure thing. Why don't you two come into the office in the morning? We'll debrief."

"Let me see when Asher's going to be released. I'll give you a call in the morning?"

"Sounds like a plan."

The day dawned wet and overcast. The temperatures were a good twenty degrees cooler than the day before. It was all we could do to get Caphy and Ethel Squeaks to go outside to do their business before we left for the Sheriff's Office. Finally, we had to bribe them with donuts before they'd comply.

We left Caphy sprawled outside Ethel Squeak's tent, her watchful gaze locked on the opening between the flaps. She lay unmoving, her head resting on her paws as the pig snorfled the last of her powdered sugar donut. Caphy had inhaled hers in seconds, but the pig liked to savor her treats. I was convinced she just liked torturing the pibl.

The sweet was a rare treat for both of them. Though at Christmas, they generally begged, borrowed, or stole five times the sugar and calories than I got, so it wasn't an altogether new experience. And when the two chow-hounds enlisted the help of the feline brains of the operation, all bets were off. The threesome could scam anything out of anyone.

I offered LaLee a bite of tuna before we left, knowing she'd stick her elegant nose up at a plebian donut.

I patted her on the head, earning myself an enraged yowl for my efforts, and followed Hal out the door.

The drive was short. The Sheriff's Office was located just off Highway 65 on the south end of town, and there was little traffic at that hour of the morning. Hal had called the hospital and spoken to Asher's doctor, who'd told us he'd be released around ten AM.

I was relieved the kid was better and coming home.

"Let's go get this over with so we can get back to normal," Hal said, his emerald green gaze holding mine in a warm embrace.

I nodded. "We need to be at the hospital at ten?"

Hal opened his door. "We don't need to pick Ash up."

"How's he going to get home then?" I asked as I climbed out of the car. My eyes were wide, and my pulse had started to pound. *Were his parents in town?*

Hal smiled.

The sky chose that moment to open up and dump copious amounts of rain on our heads. We ran toward the door and burst into the lobby, shaking ourselves like a couple of wet canines.

Arno was leaning against the Information Desk, chatting with the officer there. He straightened up as we dove through the door and glanced at his watch. "You're late."

I glared his way, and his lips twitched. He was clearly messing with me.

Arno turned on his heel and strode toward the door that divided the lobby from the heart of the station.

The place was nearly empty at that time of day. Only a couple of the deputies were at their desks.

I waved at Deputy Schmidt as she returned from the snack area with a steaming cup of coffee. She smiled, her dark blue gaze sliding appreciatively over Hal before dropping to the pile of paperwork on her desk.

Deputy Mark Sheppard was talking to a civilian. Or rather, he was searching for a pen to take what would probably amount to the crime chronicles version of War and Peace by the time the deputy finished taking all his notes.

Been there. Done that.

"Lis is here too," Arno said.

"Ame?" I asked.

Arno shoved the door of his office open. "She's at the hospital with Asher."

Relief swept through me. So that was how the kid was getting home. With the realization that I was momentarily saved from meeting my potential future in-laws, I gave Lis a wider grin than was warranted. I hugged her tight. When I drew back, I took note of the circles under her eyes and how pale she looked. "You okay?"

She nodded. "I think it all just hit me."

I took the chair nearest Lis. Hal leaned against the wall, arms crossed over his chest.

Arno sat behind his desk. He glanced at me. "Joey, you'll be happy to hear that Milo Dill admitted to being your attacker. He claimed to be looking for Asher and you got in his way."

I frowned. "Why was he looking for Asher?"

Arno and Hal shared a look.

Hal spoke first. "I didn't tell you everything about that night."

I lifted my brows. "Oh?" My tone was cool. Hal's jaw tightened at the sound.

"I'm sorry, Joey. I didn't want to worry you."

I glared at him.

Hal sighed. "Asher admitted to meeting Will in the woods that night."

"He did. I was there when he told us. So what are you keeping from me?"

"What he didn't tell us at the time, but which I

later got out of him, was that Kevin Rich was there too. Asher had given his friends your address and agreed to meet them in the woods in an attempt to work out their differences."

"Why the woods?" Lis asked.

"Asher didn't want Hal to know the boys were here," Arno said. "But he couldn't go to meet them because all he had was the 4-wheeler so they had to come to him. He was afraid if they met at the cabin, Hal might come home and catch them."

"What differences?" I asked. "You mean, because Kevin basically fingered Will to the Indy police?" I asked.

Hal nodded. "William Zola must have overheard his son talking, and he thought the boys were meeting because Dill was in town."

"Wait! You knew Dill was in town then and didn't tell me?"

"No. I only knew the boys were in the woods. But Asher insisted he was with them the whole time, and we couldn't find any reason for them to have attacked you."

I held up a hand. "My brain must be fuzzy. I don't understand. You're saying William Zola sent Milo Dill to the woods to hurt the three boys, and when he saw me he thought I was working with them?"

"As close as we can piece it together, yes," Arno said. "Except Zola didn't send him to hurt Will. That was all Dill's idea when he heard the boys were meeting there. Zola told him just to scare Asher and Kevin into remaining silent about anything they might know. But Dill had aspirations, and he saw getting rid of the boys as a good way to reach his goal. Fortunately, you and Caphy scared him off."

"What I don' t get," Hal said, "is why did Zola think the boys knew something? Asher is pretty clueless."

Arno shrugged. "I don't know for sure, but I suspect he was starting to lose confidence in Dill and it was making him paranoid. He might have suspected Will knew about what he was doing and told his friends."

"Actually," I said, "he wasn't wrong. Will did tell them he'd found drugs in their garage."

Arno nodded.

"What about the boys?" I asked. "Why didn't they help me after I was attacked?"

"They were long gone. As soon as they heard you calling Caphy, they scattered," Hal said. "You probably saved their lives."

"And your brother just left me there." The idea made me mad. Really mad.

"I know. I'm so sorry, honey. In his defense, he didn't know you were in any danger. You had Caphy, and he assumed you knew the woods well."

That logic wasn't totally faulty. I should have been okay. If Dill hadn't been there, I probably would have been. Some of the anger drained. But the kid and I would be having a talk soon.

"So, am I right in supposing that Dill killed both girls?" Hal asked Arno.

"He did. He was also the one who recruited them to sell the drugs. He promised them lots of money and things that, for a teenager who'd had a rough time in life, probably felt like the answer to everything."

Something clicked in my brain. "Rhonda Mae needed money for her mother's medical bills." A sick feeling greased my gut at the thought. "Dill's a monster."

Arno nodded. "He was good at finding weaknesses. I spoke to Mr. Gardner after the girl's body was discovered. He was totally gobsmacked by the idea that Rhonda would do something like that. But he did admit the girl had been despondent about her mother's cancer and the family's money troubles. With Rhonda Mae, Dill had an antisocial girl who needed something only he was able and willing to give her. Money for her mother's medical care. Plus, no one would suspect her of selling drugs. And she'd do anything to help her parents."

Lis made a sound of disgust. "So why did they grab Ame and me?"

Hal shook his head. "They thought they could use you to lure Joey in. With Asher taken care of in their minds, she was the last open switch they needed to close here in Deer Hollow."

"But they created a new open switch when they kidnapped us," Lis said reasonably.

Hal nodded, his expression tight. What he wouldn't tell my BFF was that Zola wouldn't have left it open for long. Everyone in that daycare would have died, including, probably either Dill or Zola.

Arno sighed. "When William Zola heard that Dill had killed another good-time girl, he came down from Indy thinking he'd have it out with the man. But after he spoke to Penn..."

"The conversation I overheard in the grocery?" I asked. A light bulb went on in my brain. "Penn wasn't telling his dad he'd kill Asher for him. He was promising to take care of Dill."

Arno nodded. "Most likely. The timing is about right. Penn told his father that Dill was going to try to kill Asher and the other boys."

"Wait!" I held up a hand again. "How did he know that?"

"He'd been following the man for days. Penn was your mystery footprint in the hotel. He'd seen Dill stalking Asher and Ame. He figured Ame another target for a good-time girl, but he knew Asher was Will Zola's friend. He put two and two together, along with some things he'd heard from the kids he'd spoken to. He realized Dill was making a play to take over."

"But if he was working for the police, why would he get his father worked up about Dill? That seems counter-productive," I said.

"He thought he could control the situation. Remember, William Zola has friends in very high places who have been protecting and would continue to protect him. The plan was to catch Dill in the act and then get him to turn on Zola. Penn told his father he was trying to keep William Zola from having fingerprints on whatever happened here. Zola is a coward, so that sounded good to him. He trusted Penn to take care of his younger son and deal with Dill," Arno said. "But Penn underestimated Dill. Things were quickly spiraling out of control and he was worried another kid would die, so Penn Zola decided he needed to make his move. He went to the campground last night to get Dill to confess. He was going to record the confession and give it to the police. But Dill figured out what he was doing. He attacked Penn and got away," Arno continued.

"We thought Penn was staying there," Hal admitted. "Junior told Joey he'd seen a campground sticker on Penn's truck."

"Now we know he probably just paid five dollars for a sticker so he could keep an eye on Dill," I added.

"How was Zola senior involved in this, exactly," Lis asked.

"He was bankrolling the operation. It was his brainchild," Hal said.

Arno nodded. "He recruited Dill as the interface to the target dealers. Unfortunately, Dill soon realized he didn't need Zola. He had the contacts, the organization was already bankrolling itself, and Zola was too afraid of being caught to be of any help at all. What Dill wasn't taking into account was that Zola has a lot of political pull in Indy. When he started to suspect that Dill was stabbing him in the back, he pulled some strings to get his oldest son in place as a CI."

"What? You mean Penn is dirty after all?"

"No. He let his father set him in place because it suited him," Arno said. "But according to Muldane, he came clean about his father from the beginning. William Zola won't escape unscathed in this. He's an accessory to the two murders and multiple counts of dealing, but he'll need to be isolated from his sponsors first. That will take some time."

Silence descended on the room for a long moment. I needed to ask about Medford but was loathe to bring his name up for obvious reasons. Finally, I realized I needed to clear the air. "How was Garland Medford involved in this? Do you think William Zola had him killed?"

Arno stared at his hands for a beat, his brow furrowed in thought. Finally, he looked up. "Milo Dill ran him off the road. He used his supposed vacation to give him an alibi, but I'm speculating that he simply drove back up to Indy to do the deed and then returned to Deer Hollow. Now that we have his car we can prove it beyond a reasonable doubt. As to how Medford was involved? Believe it or not, Muldane has spoken to witnesses who've declared that Medford was protecting the kids. Like Zola, he has friends in high places. It's possible he was killed to protect Zola, but we just don't know yet. Detective Muldane will be taking a closer look at that once she closes this case."

"I have a question," Hal said. "Any idea who put those pills in Asher's pocket?"

Arno actually smiled. "You won't believe it."

Hal cocked a brow.

"A kid named Leon Burrows bought them from the victim before she was killed. When the party-goers saw the deputies tearing up to the house, chaos ensued. Burrows used the commotion to shove the pills he'd just bought into Asher's pocket so he wouldn't get caught with them."

Hall and I shared a look and we both said, "Burrows!" with a snarl on our lips. We'd come up against the Burrows before. They were a disreputable local family with way too many kids, every one of them destined for prison.

"Did you ever get the ME's report on Rhonda Mae?" I asked.

Arno expelled an unhappy breath. "I did. From

the bruising around her mouth and face, it looks like Dill shoved the pills into her mouth before he strangled her. He clearly hoped we'd just assume it was an overdose. The poor girl didn't have a chance."

"Why?" I asked. "Why'd he kill her?"

"Because after talking to her at the diner under the false pretense of giving her a scholarship, Dill told her she would have to help him out if she wanted the money he'd promised. She agreed to sell some pills for him, but she wasn't happy. The meeting left him uneasy. He convinced himself she was going to go to the police with his story." Arno shook his head. "Dill decided to cut his losses with the girl."

Silence pulsed through the room as we all took a moment to grieve for a sweet girl who'd only wanted to help her parents with some medical bills.

After a minute, Hal pushed away from the wall. "Anything else?" he asked Arno.

The cop shook his head. "No. Lis and I are going out to breakfast. Do you two want to join us?"

I shook my head. "Raincheck? I just want to go home and put on my comfies. I'm exhausted." I stood up and Lis did too.

"I'll talk to you tomorrow," she said.

"Absolutely."

The drive home was quiet. Hal and I were both lost in our thoughts. Hal likely thought I was mad at him for not telling me everything, but I really wasn't.

After I was attacked, I hadn't been in a good place. Knowing that I hadn't just accidentally come up against someone random in my woods that night would have shaken my world even more than it already was.

"Stop by the mailbox, will you?" I asked Hal. "I don't think I grabbed the mail yesterday."

He did as I asked, pulling up close to the box at the end of my long drive. As expected, the box was full of packages and letters.

As Hal drove slowly toward my house, I tugged a fancy-looking cream-colored letter from the stack, frowning at the lack of a return address. I ripped it open and extracted a single sheet of paper, cut to fit inside the envelope without folding.

A single sentence was typed across the sheet. As I read it, my world tilted on its axis and I forgot to breathe.

Reports of my demise are greatly exaggerated. G

G for Garland? Ice painted my entire body at the meaning behind the words. Was it possible? Could Medford still be alive? No. That was crazy. If it was true, why would he write to tell me about it? Was he taunting me? Was it a threat?

"What in the world...?" Hal said, his voice sounding strained.

I thought he was talking about the note. My head jerked up, and my mouth opened to say something... anything that might warm the ice from my skin.

He wasn't looking at the letter.

I followed his gaze with my own and sucked air. Panic clawed at my already ice-encased heart.

An unfamiliar sedan was parked in front of my house. Four people sat on the porch, watching the rain fall, and our arrival.

I recognized Asher and Ame. But sitting with them was an attractive middle-aged couple who looked a lot like Ash and Hal.

A *lot* like them.

Houston, we have a problem.

The potential future in-laws have landed.

The End

READ MORE COUNTRY COUSIN MYSTERIES

If you enjoyed **Reluctant Bumpkin**, you might want to check out the rest of the series. Please enjoy Chapter One of **Humpty Bumpkin**, Book 1 of the *Country Cousin Mysteries* as my gift to you!

She's just a country girl who loves her dog. But her life is about to get less countrified and more...erm...homicide.

Deer Hollow is a small community built in a verdant, rolling countryside. The nearest big city is over an hour away, and big city ways are rejected at the Hollow. Unfortunately, the big city isn't the only place where bad things can happen.

Things like murder...which has a funny way of messin' up a debutante's day and turning a sunny Sunday in June right over onto its bucolic head.

HUMPTY BUMPKIN

The whole communication revolution thing is a mixed bag of wonderful and tedious. Things like cell phones are a revelation, allowing twenty-something women like me, who have trouble sitting still, to stay in touch with the important people in their lives while we go about our business.

But even the best innovations have their downside.

For example, a wise woman once told me never to answer a phone call whose number you don't recognize. *Answer at your own risk*, my cousin Felicity proclaimed one rainy day in the arboretum.

And I've since witnessed the intelligence of her advice. Several times over.

Unfortunately, I'm apparently a slow learner.

"Hello?"

"Is this Miss Joey Fulle?"

I frowned, not liking the "I want to sell you a bridge" tone of the caller's voice. "Nope, sorry. I think you have the wrong number."

"Actually, I believe I have the right number, Miss Fulle."

"You're not right," I said quickly and disconnected before the man on the other end of the phone had a chance to give me bad news. I had no idea what kind of bad news I was expecting. But I knew it was there, lurking like a vulture in a tree, ugly and ravenous.

I tugged the soft twisty off my shoulder-length red-blonde hair and reached up to smooth the hair back into my favorite style, which was a high ponytail. Sweat dripped down between my shoulder blades, and I was glad I'd dressed for the heat of an early June morning. Though my plain white tank top and cut off jean short shorts were already damp.

My dog, Cacophony, Caphy for short, bounded up and stopped in front of me, a clump of fur between her jaws. I grimaced. "Caphy, what did you do? Have you killed something again?"

A blonde Pitbull with gorgeous green eyes, Caphy bounced several times, her muscular haunches springing her several inches off the ground each time, and then barked happily and ran off again, tail whipping the air. I sighed, knowing I should follow her and see if I could save whatever she'd decided to "play" with.

My phone rang again. I hit *Ignore* and trudged after my dog. "Caphy girl, where'd you go?"

The distant sound of barking drew me to a copse of old trees, their gnarled branches bigger around than I was and tangled together high overhead. It was behind one of these, an elegant old Elm tree whose knobby arms spread wider than the rest, that my dog was mostly hidden. I could see her butt wagging happily as she moved around behind the tree.

"Caphy, come!"

My sweet Pitty bounced out from behind the distant tree and grinned at me, her entire body vibrating with excitement. "What have you found, girl?" I murmured to myself. "Come on, Caphy."

But she turned back to whatever she was exploring. That was when I realized she must have cornered something. I picked up the pace and hurried in her direction.

By the time I was fifteen feet away, I smelled something rotting and knew that, whatever she'd found, I wouldn't be saving it.

Real panic set in. "Caphy, you come here right now!"

My dog disappeared behind the tree, and I growled with frustration. But a moment later, she reappeared, heading in my direction with something hanging out of her mouth. "Ugh!" I fought an impulse to turn and run. Being corpse-woman was not tops on my list of favorite things.

In fact, I was pretty sure it wasn't on the list at all. "Drop it, Cacophony."

Of course she ignored me, her steps becoming bouncier and more excited the closer she came. Clearly, she wanted to share her treasure with me. I didn't know how to impress upon her that having a mangled, half-dried corpse of a bunny or squirrel dropped on my shoes didn't take me to my happy place. My usual response of shrieking and running screaming away from her treasure just didn't seem to be doing much to teach her.

She was a very bull-headed pitty. I grinned at my pun.

Caphy ran up and dropped to her haunches a few feet away. She kept hold of the object, which I was trying hard not to look at, as if she was afraid I was going to take it away from her. She would be right about that. But it wasn't going to happen until I had a bag or something to use so I didn't have to touch it. I tried one more time to get her to let loose of whatever she was clutching between her jaws. "Drop it, girl." If I was really lucky, I could convince her to let go of it and I could drag her home.

To my shock, she lowered her head and released the contents of her mouth.

I glanced down. My stomach did a painful little dance, and my gag reflex kicked in. Caphy was watching me very carefully, letting the object lie there as if checking to see how I would react. I was glad it was out of her mouth.

In fact, I would have been elated about it.

But I was too busy shrieking and running away. It might not work for her...but it worked just fine for me.

———

Deputy Arno Willager peered toward the object hulking under the trees. Two, skinny white stick-like things protruded from one end, their bony lengths painted in red streaks. He narrowed his dark brown gaze at the thing, no doubt gawking at the enormous feet on the end of the sticks.

I shuddered beside him, my dog vibrating excitedly next to me on a leash.

"Is this your chipper, Joey?"

I gave him the full force of my hostile blue gaze. "Uh, no, Deputy Willager. It's not my chipper. And, before you ask, that's not my body either."

He lifted a golden eyebrow and quirked wide lips as he skimmed my own personal body a long, slow look. "Oh, I can see that."

I frowned but didn't scold him for giving me the once over. I was on uneven ground with that one because I was pretty sure there'd been one time at a party in high school when I'd been in a closet with

Arno, our star quarterback at the time. We'd been pretty drunk and the details of what we'd been doing in there were vague. I decided that changing the subject might be a good idea. "Do you know..." I swallowed hard. "—who it is?"

Arno wrinkled his nose. "Can't be more than a couple people around here with feet that big."

I nodded, covering my nose with a hand as a warm breeze carried the butcher shop stench in our direction. "It's horrible."

Arno didn't respond. Finally, I looked at him. "Did you call Doctor Miller?"

"I did."

"Well, that's good." I glanced down at the item on the ground a few feet away. It was part of a hand. A man's hand if size was any indication. The ends of the fingers were missing, and my stomach roiled.

"Tell me how you found it."

"I told you already. "

"Humor me, Joey."

I sighed. "Caphy and I were taking a walk. It's a nice day."

He scoured me a look and I fought a grin. He was just too easy to annoy for his own good. "Caphy ran up ahead and came back with fur in her mouth."

"Fur?"

"Well...I thought it was fur. But clearly, it wasn't." My gaze skimmed to the small patch of scalp resting in the dirt where Caphy had dropped it.

"Did you walk up to the chipper?"

"No."

"You didn't touch anything? Move the body parts...?"

"Ew! Of course not. Why would you even ask me that?"

"It's my job."

Frustration twanged my last nerve. Arno had always been a man of few words, but he had to know I had about a thousand questions. As if reading my mind, he turned to frown down at me. The sun dropped slowly behind him, forming a backdrop for his tall, lean frame, narrow hips and broad shoulders. Arno's face was classically handsome, with a clean-shaven square jaw, sexy brown eyes and a pleasantly-shaped mouth with a slightly fuller lower lip that was immensely appealing. Two lines rode the space between his dense golden brows as he looked at me. He was clearly chewing on something he thought he should tell me.

"What is it, Arno?"

The worry lines deepened and he held my gaze with a searching one. "You can't talk about this, Joey. This is an ongoing investigation and I need you to promise me you won't spill details around town."

"I don't know any details."

"You know more right now than anybody else except the killer." He lifted a golden brow for emphasis.

His words finally sank in. "Oh. Yikes."

"I need you to keep a low profile until we figure out what's going on."

"Surely, this is someone from outside the *Hollow*."

He shrugged. "We don't know that yet."

I fell silent, chewing my bottom lip as a distant rumbling noise climbed ever closer to the spot where we stood. That would be Doctor Miller and the deputies Arno had called. They would have left their cars on the road and were approaching on all-terrain vehicles. My family's property included well over a hundred acres without roads. And the spot where Arno and I stood was in the most remote section of it all. The killer couldn't have found a more private spot to stick some poor schmoe into a wood chipper.

Finally, I nodded. "Okay. I promise."

"Good. Now you should get on home with that dog. She's disrupted the crime scene enough."

Caphy whined softly and dropped to her wide haunches, plying the deputy with a grin and soft eyes for good measure.

She wrung a grin out of him and he reached out to scratch the wide spot between her eyes. "You're a good girl, Caphy."

My pitty leaped to her feet and started wagging from her nose to the deadly whip of her tail, which unfortunately was smacking painfully against my leg.

I gave her leash a tug and, with one final look at the horror between the trees, we started back toward home. Despite my promise to keep the body in the chipper to myself, I had no intention of doing it. Whoever that poor soul was, he or she was killed on my property.

That made it personal.

And, personally, I didn't like it when people started flinging other people into wood chippers in my woods.

It was rude and disturbing.

And nipping it in the bud as quickly as possible seemed like the logical thing to do.

Check out the entire series here: https://samcheever.com/books/#Country

MORE BY SAM CHEEVER

Check out Sam's other bestselling series on the **BOOKS** page at https://samcheever.com/

Country Cousin Mysteries **(More fun stories with Joey, Hal, Caphy, LaLee, and Ethel Squeaks)**
Silver Hills Cozy Mysteries
Gainfully Employed Mysteries
Enchanted Inquiries Paranormal Mysteries
Reluctant Familiar Paranormal Mysteries
Yesterday's Paranormal Mysteries

ABOUT THE AUTHOR

Multiple-time *USA Today* and *Wall Street Journal* Bestselling Author Sam Cheever writes mystery and suspense, creating stories that draw you in and keep you eagerly turning pages. Known for writing great characters, snappy dialogue, and unique and exhilarating stories, Sam is the award-winning author of 80+ books.